Brandon Eggleston

JOHN DARNIELLE's first novel, *Wolf in White Van*, was a *New York Times* bestseller, a National Book Award nominee, and a finalist for the Los Angeles Times Book Prize for first fiction, and was widely hailed as one of the best novels of the year. He is a writer, composer, guitarist, and vocalist for the band the Mountain Goats. He lives in Durham, North Carolina, with his wife and sons.

ALSO BY JOHN DARNIELLE

Wolf in White Van

UNIVERSAL HARVESTER

JOHN DARNIELLE

PICADOR

FARRAR, STRAUS AND GIROUX

NEW YORK

UNIVERSAL HARVESTER. Copyright © 2017 by John Darnielle. All rights reserved. Printed in the United States of America. For information, address Picador, 175 Fifth Avenue, New York, N.Y. 10010.

picadorusa.com • picadorbookroom.tumblr.com
twitter.com/picadorusa • facebook.com/picadorusa

Picador® is a U.S. registered trademark and is used by Macmillan Publishing Group, LLC, under license from Pan Books Limited.

For book club information, please visit facebook.com/picadorbookclub or email marketing@picadorusa.com.

Designed by Abby Kagan

The Library of Congress has cataloged the Farrar, Straus and Giroux edition as follows:

Names: Darnielle, John, author.
Title: Universal harvester / John Darnielle.
Description: First edition. | New York: Farrar, Straus and Giroux. 2017.
Identifiers: LCCN 2016025809 | ISBN 9780374282103 (hardcover) | ISBN 9780374714024 (ebook)
Subjects: | BISAC: FICTION / Literary. | FICTION / Horror. | GSAFD: Horror fiction.
Classification: LCC PS3604.A748 U55 2017 | DDC 813'.6—dc23
LC record available at https://lccn.loc.gov/2016025809

Picador Paperback ISBN 978-1-250-15999-1

Our books may be purchased in bulk for promotional, educational, or business use. Please contact your local bookseller or the Macmillan Corporate and Premium Sales Department at 1-800-221-7945, extension 5442, or by email at MacmillanSpecialMarkets@macmillan.com.

First published by Farrar, Straus and Giroux

First Picador Edition: February 2018

10 9

to Nancy Chavanothai: in loving memory

But secret agents, like God, only give signs to their confidants. They are also very cruel and even unhappy at times. At any rate, they keep quiet.

—**BENJAMIN TAMMUZ,** *Minotaur,* translated from the Hebrew by Kim Parfitt and Mildred Budny

PART ONE

*

1   People usually didn't say anything when they returned their tapes to the Video Hut: in a single and somewhat graceful movement, they'd approach the counter, slide the tapes toward whoever was stationed behind the register, and wheel back toward the door. Sometimes they'd give a wordless nod or raise their eyebrows a little to make sure they'd been seen. With a few variations, this silent pass was the unwritten protocol at video rental stores around the U.S. for the better part of two decades. Some stores had slots in the counter that dropped into a big bin, but Nevada was a small town. A little cleared space off to the side of the counter was good enough.

Bob Pietsch was renting *Advanced Big Game* and *Best of Bass Fishing Volume Four* today; he stood there now, at the counter, patient, semimonolithic. He stopped in sometimes on his way home from the co-op; any tapes he rented he'd keep for a week. Stephanie Parsons was in line behind him; Jeremy could see her back there, looking mildly anxious, but there wasn't much he could do about it.

Bob spent most of the year by himself in a farmhouse on a property he owned outside Collins. If he still hunted or fished, it wasn't with anybody he'd known back when he lived in town: nobody really knew what Bob did with his time. People talked a little about him, out there all by himself; it was hoped he'd remarry. But he'd sold the family home after his wife died, and the Collins place was pretty remote. There weren't a lot of opportunities to meet people. When he made conversation these days he sounded like a farmer at an auction waiting for the bidding to start.

"This one's a real good one," he said, tapping *Best of Bass Fishing Volume Four*. "They get smallmouth, they have to throw half of them back."

"Ever get up to Hickory Grove?" Jeremy asked him. He had lived in Iowa all his life. Men in his family always talked about fishing.

"Used to. All the time," said Bob. "We used to go out for bluegill in the winter."

"Sure," said Jeremy. It continued like this for a minute. Bob eventually dug his Video Hut membership card out from behind his driver's license and signed for the tapes. His card was one of the old laminated ones; it had gone yellow at the edges. Membership cards were really a formality at this point, but Jeremy let him show it anyway.

Stephanie waited as Bob made his way slowly past the shelves and out the door before stepping up to the counter. She didn't set her tape down; instead, she held it in her hand, chest-high, a little away from her body.

"There's something on this one," she said.

Jeremy reached for the tape; he recognized it. He'd circled its title when the distributor's catalog was making the rounds about a year ago. Everybody who worked the counter had a say in what got ordered; Sarah Jane, who owned the place, had implemented this system when she took over from the previous owner. She was

4

privately proud about it. As a younger woman she'd worked retail for years.

"Oh, yeah," he said, turning toward the shelves behind him, several hundred videotapes in clear cases and a few dozen in translucent pink: soft adult movies that hardly anybody ever rented. "Sorry. It sounded really good in the catalog but it's really old, right?" It was called *Targets*. It had Boris Karloff.

Stephanie looked a little blankly at Jeremy, measuring him, then said: "No, it's a great movie, I've seen it before. At school." Stephanie'd taken a masters in education from the University of Chicago; she made mention of it when she could. "It's the tape, there's something on it."

"I can credit your account," said Jeremy.

Stephanie put on her measuring face again and seemed to decide Jeremy wasn't going to understand. "No, it's fine," she said. "Never mind. Maybe tell Sarah Jane about it, though, OK?"

"Sure thing," said Jeremy. He felt stupid: he wasn't stupid, but he found Stephanie intimidating, and he didn't know how to talk to her. He told himself as he put the display case back on the rack that he'd remember, but he closed the store himself that night, and didn't see Sarah Jane until Monday, and by then he had forgotten.

Steve Heldt was reattaching a rain gutter to the awning over the front door when Jeremy got home after dark; he'd turned on the floodlight on the side of the garage. His breath in the glare made giant clouds.

Jeremy parked in the driveway and stepped out. "Maybe wait until morning?" he said. His voice came out solitary, singular in the February air. Dad was in his boots up on the ladder, continuously adjusting his perch as he worked.

"Not today, big man," Steve said. Jeremy'd been "big man" ever since the day he'd helped his father change a tire when he was eight years old. "It's going to snow all night. If it warms up after noon this thing'll fall right off."

The gutter wasn't going to fall right off if they waited until daylight to fix it: Steve knew it, Jeremy knew it. But they also both knew to keep busy in winter if they could. Mom had gone off new Highway 30 into a telephone pole in the snow six years ago, in 1994. Jeremy'd been sixteen.

He put his gloves back on and held the ladder while his dad drove in the nails. There wasn't much wind but a little breeze, maybe; it moved the snow around at his feet. "Get home late today?" he said.

"No," said Steve. "Just didn't think of it until after dark. Saw the forecast." Then there wasn't much else to say, and the hammer pounding dully became the only sound you could hear in the neighborhood besides the occasional creak of a branch.

Later on they watched *Reindeer Games*: Jeremy brought home new releases when they were something his dad might like. Spy stuff. Cop movies, sometimes. They got a late start because of the rain gutter; the movie wasn't over until nearly midnight.

They both found *Reindeer Games* confusing, and their attention wandered as it ran. They talked through the slow parts. Afterwards they tried to answer each other's questions about it, but they couldn't get it straight. Then Dad started in about the job.

"There's soil labs, water labs right here in town," he said.

"Dad," said Jeremy. "I have a job."

"Sure. Not a whole lot in it, though, you know."

"I know." He picked up the remote and hit REWIND. "You're right. I don't know."

"Well, I saw some postings, anyway."

"I was thinking about starting DMACC next semester."

"Well, you said that last year, though."

The VCR auto-ejected and Jeremy put the tape back into its case. "I know," he said. "You're right."

In some versions of this story, there's an argument here, because Jeremy feels like his father is being nosy, and because he feels ashamed of being twenty-two years old and not having made anything of himself yet; he's resentful when something reminds him about it. In these variations Jeremy tells his father to give him a little breathing room, and Steve Heldt, who is a good father and who shares, with his son, an incapacitating loss, thinks to himself: *Stay out of your son's way; he'll find his way if you let him.* In some other versions Jeremy stays awake for a couple of hours, maybe watching another movie he brought home but unable to focus on it, and in the morning he tells his father to write down some of those job listings, and he ends up getting a position at a soil testing lab in Newton, eventually transferring to a bigger lab back home in Nevada.

In this version he keeps his job at the Video Hut, and then something else happens.

2   Story County was prairie until the mid-1800s. In school they taught a little about the Iowa tribes, but it was hard to get a clear picture of who exactly'd been in Story County when the settlers got there. There had to have been somebody, though. That word *Iowa*, that was a native word, and lots of places throughout the state were named after tribes: Sioux City. Tama. Black Hawk. Plus it was a known thing that tribes had been removed from their land all over the state at some point during the westward expansion. But they didn't really dwell on this too much in high school, so all Jeremy really had was a rough outline. Few details, or none.

About his own family, where they were from, he knew a little more; when his grandparents or his aunts and uncles got together on the Fourth of July or Thanksgiving it was pretty much all they talked about. All conversations tended toward simple genealogy and geography: who was related to whom, who lived where now, where they'd lived in the first place. There was a numbing comfort to it. These conversations, endlessly repeatable at any family gathering, were a zero-stakes game. Is Pete still in Tama? No, he got a job over in Marshalltown working in sales for Lennox. Is that the air-conditioning people? Well, Pete says "climate control." Oh, "climate control," is that it? Sure, sure.

Tracing of movements was the whole of the process. If the recruiter from Caterpillar collared Mike at the job fair and offered to double his salary inside of two years, then that was how Mike and his family ended up in Peoria: but simple movement atop a shared, internalized map was still the heart of the action, the desired point of engagement. Bill's up in Storm Lake now. Did he sell the Urbandale place? The place off Seventy-second? No, that was a rental. Oh, is that right? Yes, the Handsakers owned it, they rented it out for years until their youngest got back from Coe. You mean Davy? Well, but he goes by Dave now. From Davy to Dave to Dave's parents to their folks you could get a fair bit of talking done, but the trail went cold at about that point. Jeremy's mom's grandparents were Russian somehow, one of those places that wasn't really Russia any more. His great-grandfather on his dad's side had come from Germany. But it went no further than that. The tracking of local movements was sufficient work until it came time to part ways, and they'd pick up where they left off at Labor Day, or Christmas.

By the time he was fourteen, Jeremy could locate magnetic north from practically any place in Story County, even in the total absence of known landmarks. Knowing where you were: this seemed like a big part of the point of living in Nevada, possibly of being alive at all. In the movies, people almost never talked about the towns they spent their lives in; they ran around having adventures and never stopped to get their bearings. It was weird, when you thought about it. They only remembered where they were from if they wanted to complain about how awful it was there, or, later, to remember it as a place of infinite promise, a place whose light had been hidden from them until it became unrecoverable, at which point its gleam would become impossible to resist.

Video Hut opened at ten in the morning, which was ridiculous. Anybody returning tapes before mid-afternoon just used the slot in the door, and hardly anybody ever came in to rent before noon at the earliest. Still, there'd be one person sitting behind the counter just in case, waiting for the store's day to actually begin. Sometimes hours would pass.

There was a television mounted above the racks in one corner of the store. During shop hours it showed movies continuously. By policy, these had to be movies with a PG rating or lower. Picking out the movie and starting it up was one of the duties listed on the A.M. OPEN sheet, a six-point list printed on neon-green paper and affixed to the counter by the register with clear tape whose corners had frayed and blackened over the years:

1. lights front and back
2. power up register
3. count cash on hand in strongbox, record in notebook and move to register
4. file slot returns, return cases to displays
5. pick tape (PG or lower) for in-store, start up computer
6. check database for tapes overdue 3+plus days and make phone calls

The list was there to make the opening routine look like work, though in practice it took Jeremy about five minutes altogether. He went to the computer before even turning on the lights; it was a Gateway 2000. Gateway'd still been a more or less local company when the computer was new; it creaked through its start-up routine for a full five minutes now. By the time it was ready to use, Jeremy'd gone through everything else on the list except the overdues. He wasn't going to call anybody about overdues before noon, anyway.

Underneath the counter there were six or seven tapes that got played in rotation—this was the "pick tape" step, almost entirely mechanical. *The Muppet Movie, Bugsy Malone, A League of Their Own, Star Wars*: most people working the opening shift just grabbed one without looking. There were a couple of newer ones that got traded in and out from month to month. Jeremy usually went for these, keeping the sound muted until customers started showing up.

He had *Reindeer Games* in his hand when he got to the store, so he put it on with the sound down and paid it no mind, letting it run while he leafed through a summer courses catalog from DMACC. Joan from Mary Greeley stopped in to trade out a couple of exercise tapes for new ones; the hospital got these tapes for free, which was fine, since nobody else rented them. Joan used them for classes on the convalescent ward. She came up to the counter and nodded over her shoulder toward the screen overhead: the picture went black and white for a second as Jeremy looked up, then stabilized.

"Not expecting a lot of customers today?" she said. Charlize Theron was in a swimming pool untying her bikini.

"What? Oh. Sorry, sorry," said Jeremy, reaching for the remote. Joan laughed. "No, it's fine." He stopped the tape just as things were starting to get explicit. "Sorry, I watched this last night, I don't know what I was thinking."

"It's fine," said Joan again, nodding encouragingly; Jeremy's face was flushed. "I'm forty-six, I've seen it all before."

"No, I know, I just—wasn't thinking," he said. He grabbed the two new exercise tapes from the shelf, brow still furrowed.

"You OK?"

"Yeah, yeah," he said, shaking his head like a cat waking up. "I don't think I slept well. Fell asleep on the couch."

"Happens to me all the time!" said Joan, signing the rental slip with its crossed-through zero in the "amount" column and sliding her new tapes into her puffy oversized purse.

"Yeah," said Jeremy, "me, too," which wasn't true. Neither was the part about falling asleep on the couch; he didn't know why he'd said it. He was off his rhythm.

"See you next week," said Joan.

"All right," said Jeremy, and that sounded wrong, too.

The rest of the day was a winter day at a video store in the late 1990s: long stretches without any customers, a big rush between 5:30 and 7:00 as people were getting off work and heading home, and then the slowdown. Lindsey Redinius brought back a copy of *She's All That* during the rush and said there was something wrong with it, that the movie cut out at some point, turned into something different and came back later. Jeremy set it aside. This was the second complaint about a tape in two days. Maybe they were making tapes from cheaper materials now? DVD players were supposed to be the next thing.

He looked around the store as he was shutting down. It was a heated Morton building, same materials they used for barns now: the same building exactly, just with different stuff in it. In the dark you could see how temporary it was. He rifled through the returns bin and grabbed another tape in case he couldn't sleep, and he stopped at Taco John's up the street for a family value pack. Then he got onto old Highway 30 and headed for home.

They'd plowed the road earlier that morning and several times throughout the afternoon. Everyone was driving a little slower, to be careful. This was the feel of the season for Jeremy. Slow cars moving over icy roads in the dark. Heavy branches on trees. Headlights. Mute and palpable, the melancholy would last at least through March. There was a melody to it you could catch if you weren't trying too hard.

Dad was already home when he got there; they ate their tacos at the dinner table, like a family.

3   "Everything OK at work?"

"Sure. Big contract from a firm in Minnesota building a new motel over in Ames."

"Yeah?"

"Just a Holiday Inn Express. They need everything at once, want to be up and running in time for Big 12." Jeremy kept it to himself, but he was happy to hear his dad would be busy all winter, coordinating orders of resin from competing suppliers and ordering his team around, shipping pipe out on flatbeds. Dad seemed happiest when he was busy enough to be worn out by the end of the day.

"Downtown?"

"No, out by I-35. All kinds of new stuff going up over there," he said; Steve Heldt didn't think Ames really had any more room to expand, but they kept building stuff just in case. "Big contract, anyway."

Jeremy cleared the table; there wasn't much to it, just throwing away some trash. He leaned over his shoulder and said "Beast?" while opening the refrigerator; this was shorthand for beer in the Heldt house. Steve held himself to one beer after dinner; how he'd settled on Milwaukee's Best was lost to history, but the alliance was permanent. Years ago, Mom had brought a six-pack of Stroh's home once when it was all she saw on the shelf at Fareway. It sat in the refrigerator for a solid year.

He tossed the can to his dad underhand and they both headed to the living room: it was the pattern during winter. In summer, they had a lot of fun together grilling out back, but neither man had really ever taken to the kitchen. They didn't feel at home in there. It still felt like it belonged to Mom.

They watched *Proof of Life* that night, the one Jeremy'd grabbed without looking. They both enjoyed it. There was comfort and ease in watching movies together; Jeremy considered himself a little more high-minded than his dad, but they both disappeared into the screen's glow at about the same time, and they stayed lost once they got there. The room filled with light. It was a space they could share, something to be grateful for without having to think too much about it.

Dad went to bed immediately afterward—"See you tomorrow," he said, like a coworker leaving early—but Jeremy stayed up to give *She's All That* a look. He knew tapes to break down over time, but when it happened people didn't usually elaborate on it. The tape's chewed up about halfway through, they'd say. You can see something's going to happen about a minute before and then the machine spits it out, they'd say. It makes a squiggly noise.

This was different. Twice now people'd brought in tapes, different ones, and said there was something on the actual tape that didn't belong. Something they'd watched through and come out on the other side of. They seemed confused trying to describe it; either they hadn't wanted to go into detail, or they didn't know how. "There's another movie that was on this tape," was how Lindsey'd put it. "They must have recorded over the old one."

She's All That wasn't something Jeremy would have otherwise watched on his own. It was boring. He felt restless on the couch, picking stray threads from cushions, following a plot that didn't interest him, debating whether to reheat the remaining Potato Olés. Fifteen minutes in he realized he could have checked Stephanie Parsons's copy of *Targets* instead, and he felt annoyed with himself; he thought about just heading off to bed. But then, in the middle of a scene where a crying woman was typing something onto a computer terminal, the television screen blinked dark for a half second; and then it went light again, and Jeremy sat up straight, and found himself watching a black-and-white scene, shot by a single camera, mounted or held by a very steady hand. At first, he had to turn the volume up to hear whether there was even any sound at all: there was, but not much. A little wind across the camera's microphone, the audible rise and fall of a person breathing. There was a timecode in the corner scrolling along. The date read 00/00/0000. There didn't seem to be much else to see, but then the breathing sound quickened and movements began breaking roughly through the dark.

The scene lasted about four minutes. Then the screen twitched again, and *She's All That* roared back into the room from the silence, while Jeremy, now wide awake and fully focused, stared at the action as if waiting for somebody to break character and maybe explain to the camera what everybody'd just seen.

But he knew that wasn't actually going to happen. Somebody had transferred a scene onto *She's All That*. Weren't tapes somehow protected against people copying stuff onto them? But there had to be some way of getting around it. He watched on without listening, waiting for a third blink that might put the first two into clearer context, but nothing came. After twenty minutes he thought about rewinding. He decided instead to fast forward without

16

pushing STOP. The action developed wordlessly now, but all in color, all the right movie.

He hit REWIND once the end credits started to roll, and he watched the black-and-white scene again, and then a third time; finally he went back to his bedroom and tried to sleep, with limited success.

The quiet of the snow out in the yard early the next day: it was probably the best thing about winter, these mornings with their open stillnesses. Jeremy had slept badly and was up before the sun, thinking about watching *She's All That* again, wondering whether he should show it to his dad. But he decided to forget it. Someone had taped something personal onto a movie they'd rented: that wasn't supposed to be possible, but maybe it was; who'd ever tried, but who cared?

The road out to the Lincoln Highway didn't get plowed until mid-afternoon. Jeremy had to call in late. He got to work around two. Sarah Jane was on her stool by the computer, doing a crossword puzzle.

"I should have called you and told you to stay home," she said. "Nobody's coming in till they finish plowing side streets."

He stood at the door kicking the remaining snow off his shoes. "It's all right," he said.

"You feel like working the same shift tomorrow?" she asked him as he was getting settled. "I don't want to make Ezra drive home over these roads after dark." Ezra lived with his mother and father south of Ames on a property as old as any in the area; he had to drive over half a mile of gravel road to get to the highway, in a car that was barely up to the task. His father had offered to help him out with a down payment on something sturdier, but

Ezra, though only nineteen, felt a deep aversion to debt, and a deeper one to casting any tool aside that had any use left in it. Farm kids are like this, I've found. They don't like throwing useful things away.

"No problem," Jeremy said. It was how he'd been raised.

"Pizza?" She gestured toward a Casey's box on the counter.

"Sure," said Jeremy. He knew he should eat better, but he didn't ever get around to trying. He pulled up a stool and set his backpack down, and he looked up at the screen; Sarah Jane was watching the news, which was all about the weather, which roads were open and which ones weren't, how long it was going to take to drive from Des Moines to Urbandale or Ankeny to Clive.

"Hey, a customer complained about this one so I took it home," he said after a while, wiping his hand on his jeans. "Somebody taped over onto it."

"Somebody what?"

"Taped over it. It's got some scene in a barn with these people in it. Kinda freaked me out."

She reached over for the tape and looked at it as if it might reveal something right then and there. "Don't these have erase tabs?"

"I don't know," said Jeremy. "I didn't think you could tape over 'em, anyway."

"Well, I'll have a look," said Sarah Jane, and she got up and went off to the break room, which wasn't big enough for anybody to really take breaks in and so served as a coat closet. Jeremy thought for a second to suggest that they look at it in the store, but then considered that he didn't really want to see it again, and that it wasn't his problem any further than to report it to his boss.

There was a pretty decent rush of customers toward four o'clock: people who'd made it into work but expected to be home all the weekend. They were stocking up on things to watch. The Kids and Family section was nearly empty by 5:30, and then the stampede died down. Sarah Jane went home and said Jeremy could close early if he wanted, but he stuck it out until 9:00. He didn't mind an empty store. Better to drive home when there were fewer people on the roads.

4   *Targets* is a film by Peter Bogdanovich. Released in 1968, it tracks two lives about to intersect: Byron Orlok, an aging film icon in the twilight of his career, played by Boris Karloff, and Bobby Thompson, a young soldier recently home from Vietnam, played by Tim O'Kelly, who also played Danno in the pilot episode of *Hawaii Five-O.*

Karloff was eighty years old when he landed the role of Byron Orlok. Contracted to shoot for two days, he liked the script so well that when an additional three days were needed to complete his scenes, he worked without pay. His performance represents a victory of human will over stubborn flesh; suffering from emphysema and rheumatoid arthritis, wearing braces on his legs, able to walk or stand only with the help of a cane, Karloff acts his way through these obstacles of ill health and old age. Orlok, like the actor, is a surviving remnant of a bygone age; the monsters he played when he was younger and stronger have given way to the ongoing shocks of the late twentieth century, to atrocities of war and the isolation of modern life. There are new monsters now.

In *Targets*, the monster is Bobby, who, without any identifiable provocation, kills half his family and a deliveryman after breakfast one morning, then gets into his car and takes to the road. Climbing an oil tank by an abandoned amusement park, from a perch overlooking the freeway, he eats lunch, drinks a Coca-Cola, and then snipes, emotionless, at the speeding cars below; located and then pursued by police, he flees, seeking cover at a drive-in theater.

The film's climax follows. From a hiding place inside the drive-in's screen, he takes aim at patrons in their cars. He hits one man in a phone booth; he gets another at the concession stand. Outraged filmgoers, some armed, storm down the asphalt. In attendance for the premiere of *The Terror*, his swan song, Orlok exits his limousine, and, in the half-darkness of the projection booth, encounters Bobby. A struggle follows; the older man disarms the younger with his cane. As the police lead the shooter away in handcuffs, he wonders aloud how high his kill tally will run, and if he'll be on the evening news.

The VHS copy of *Targets* in the racks at Video Hut features two scenes not present on the original print. The first of these is brief, and profoundly empty: it's a stationary view of a chair that sits in the corner of an outbuilding somewhere, maybe a barn or toolshed. Without any external cues it's hard to say. There's a workbench partially visible at the left of the frame, or a sawhorse; this view holds for two silent minutes, fairly steady. Halfway through, there's a momentary jerk, like a sweaty thumb slipping from the camera's housing, but other than this there is no action to describe. The chair, the corner of something; behind the chair, a wall, corrugated aluminum or tin. There's sound, but nobody makes any noise. Microphone hiss serves to indicate that the air was still and quiet within the walls where the scene was shot.

The second scene is longer. It again features the chair in the outbuilding, but there's a person sitting in it now. She, or he, wears a canvas bag for a hood; some yellow vinyl-coated polypropylene rope attaches the bag to her head at the neck. Clad in a billowing T-shirt and jeans, the chair lady could be anybody: there's no way of placing her in any external context. You might think, when you first see her, that she's bound to her chair; the hood and the rope suggest captivity, confinement, restraint. Her hands are behind her. But then she rises to her feet, or he to his, it makes no difference and it's impossible to tell, and raises both arms from behind her back up and over her head, hands held like claws, fingers splayed and pointed downward as one poised to descend onto the keys of a piano or shoot lightning bolts at the ground. Slowly, she lifts her left foot; her right knee quivers, and half-buckles, but she holds the pose.

She stands that way for several minutes. When her balance wavers, she rights it, through some unmeasurable calibration of tendon and muscle; her effort, her focus, is palpable. You can hear the sound of her feet on the straw when she shifts, a corrective stutter. You can also hear the sleeve of someone's jacket brushing against the camera's built-in microphone. If you happen to have the volume up high enough, you can even hear the sound when the hand emerges from behind the lens and juts into the frame. There. *Skkitch.*

It holds a paintbrush. The camera advances, presumably held by the painter's other hand: in close-up now, the head inside the canvas bag breathes audibly, steady, a little labored. The hand starts painting something on the canvas hood: it paints where the eyes would be, but makes them exaggerated, grotesque, unlifelike. A caricature. It daubs mindlessly once or twice on the left cheek, leaving an incoherent blotch. Toward the forehead it begins lines that might become letters—there's an angle, possibly the initial strokes of an N, or an M, or an A. V, maybe. Then the frame shakes, and the door to the outbuilding, ajar and opening onto a yard, comes into view for a second before the camera jolts back into the building.

It stops before it gets back to the risen figure. There's nothing in the frame now but the wall, which then wheels, upended, and we're either looking at the ceiling or the floor.

Somebody says: "Wait. I didn't—"

Then *Targets* resumes, right in the middle of the action by the freeway, Bobby sniping blankly away, heading down to the destiny from which no one can rescue him, unless you want to rewind and watch the outbuilding scene again, which you might, maybe twice even, in case you missed something, maybe a fingernail, or a boot, or an errant swatch of hair.

It was several weeks before Jeremy watched *Targets*, as it turned out. Sarah Jane hadn't said anything to him about *She's All That*, because while she'd remembered to take it home, she hadn't gotten around to watching it. She didn't mind being in her forties as much as she'd expected to: but she needed to write things down now in order to remember them, and she resented that. Twenty years ago she'd been so attentive to detail; nothing got past her. When, after a few days, she spotted the tape looking neglected underneath a few stray pieces of unopened junk mail, she scowled. She'd returned it to the racks in the store without mentioning it to Jeremy.

Jeremy still bristled when he remembered *Targets*, meanwhile, but he'd managed to prevent any actual questions from coalescing around his vague unease. *She's All That* was a dud: nobody was renting it. So his radar'd stayed clear long enough for the memory to recede painlessly into the past, where unanswered questions starved quietly to death.

Except then one day Stephanie Parsons came in, wearing a jade-green jacket and looking like a substitute teacher. To Jeremy she looked great; he was beginning to remember his high school days fondly.

"Did you ever have a look at that copy of *Targets*?" she asked at the counter.

"Oh, hey," said Jeremy. "I am real sorry. I think I—"

"Did Sarah Jane?"

"I guess," said Jeremy. "I told her about it. She took it home."

Stephanie looked at him: when Jeremy met her gaze he anticipated anger, but there was more in there. He could see her making calculations.

"I'd really like for one of you to have a look at it," she said after a moment. "It keeps bothering me."

"Yeah, OK," he said. "I'll check it out tonight."

She looked behind her toward the small space of the store, which was empty. "Can we look at it in here?"

"We're only supposed to play certain stuff when the store's open," he said.

Stephanie scratched an itch on her cheek. "Can we just look at it in here?"

It wasn't like he was going to get fired, and it didn't matter anyway. Nobody was going to start coming in for at least another hour and a half. He located the tape and loaded it into the in-store VCR, and he let it run.

They stood there watching, heads tilted back, looking up. It wasn't really dark in the store and it wasn't especially light. It was sort of gray. This was on a Tuesday morning in March, when some of the trees were in bud, and the stray black clumps of snow that still lay on the ground looked sticky.

"Everything OK, big man?" Steve asked Jeremy at dinner. They were having fried chicken; it was Dad's signature dish and something of a tradition. The smell of hot oil in the kitchen, the sound of sizzling chicken skin, meant good things in the Heldt house. A tax rebate. A project moving forward. A hurdle jumped.

"Yeah, just some weird stuff at work."

"Weird?"

"Somebody recording over some tapes."

"Recording—?"

"Putting other stuff on them, weird stuff."

"Like, dirty movies?"

Jeremy winced a little; he didn't like to be reminded that his father was probably very lonely.

"No, just weird stuff. I brought one of them home." He tapped *Targets*, sitting atop a stack of three tapes beside his plate on the kitchen table. It would have been nice to leave it in the same locked drawer in his mind where he'd put *She's All That*. Lindsey Redinius thought her copy of *She's All That* was defective: after her account got credited for rental, she forgot all about it. Stephanie was different, so he had to follow through.

"OK," said Steve. "We'll have to check it out." Jeremy nodded without looking up from his plate, and they moved on to talking about work starting at the Ames site. He chewed his food slowly and he asked lots of questions, technical things he knew his dad would answer. He wanted dinner to last awhile, because he was hoping to avoid having to check out *Targets* with Dad.

He didn't really want to watch it again at all. He'd only taken it

25

home that night out of a sense of duty. The three hours he'd spent pausing and restarting it with Stephanie Parsons in the store seemed like enough. Maybe the interruptions of the customers coming and going had made it a little easier to bear, or maybe the constant stopping and starting had made it worse, but in either case he was hoping to shield his father from it, because it wasn't the sort of thing you wanted to bring home to your family. Underneath it on the table were *Three Days of the Condor* and *The Fourth Protocol*, intended as insurance against his father expressing any interest whatsoever in *Targets*.

They proved effective decoys. *The Fourth Protocol* was a little hard to follow, but had just enough action to make up for it. Steve Heldt said "Good night" when it was over, and Jeremy said, "See you in the morning"; but, while his father headed straight down the hall to his bedroom, Jeremy stayed where he was, on the couch in front of the television. Two hours later, he was still there, awake, staring straight ahead with his arms crossed, pausing and rewinding, trying to make out the contours of these figures so poorly lit that they kept vanishing wholly into shadow.

5   They were having lunch at Gregory's Coffee House on South Duff, over in Ames. Stephanie'd brought along a notebook with a farm scene on the cover; the picture looked like it had been taken at least forty years ago. Its finish was bright and shiny, though; maybe it had been sitting in a rack at the Ben Franklin on Sixth Street for years, just waiting. Who knows. The lines on its pages were wide-ruled, faded blue. It could have belonged to a child.

"OK," she said, flipping the cover open to a page covered with handwritten columns, each line headed by a manic asterisk. The column on the left said *She* at the top; the one on the right, *Targets*. "Here. The two scenes in *Targets* run for a total of nine minutes. The first one's nothing and I can't figure it out. The second scene you could almost think was somebody's home sex tape, but the one in *She's All That* is different but visibly in the same building, so I don't know."

"I don't know," Jeremy said. "It's so dark."

"It's the same building." She flipped two pages forward. "At the one-minute mark, when the victim bucks, she either hits the guy holding the camera or he jumps to the side, and you see the worktable."

"Miss Parsons," Jeremy said. Every time they met up he felt less inclined to call her by her first name. This was their third meeting since they'd watched *Targets* together in the store a few weeks ago; she'd rented both tapes twice in the intervening period. "I don't know if that's really . . . like, you keep saying 'victim.'"

"What do you want? 'Prisoner'?"

"I don't know." He looked down at her columns, at the question marks and exclamation points written in the margins. "I think if you think it's anything we should call the police."

"And tell them what?" She was right. The scene on *She's All That* was very hard to watch, both because the image was so dark and because the sounds were so troubling: the kicks, the fingernails scraping denim. "They'll say they're sex tapes. Bondage stuff. People's home movies."

"Well, OK, you're probably right." She was. Jeremy's dad knew the chief of police. He would not have understood why he'd been asked to look at something that made no sense on a rental tape nobody cared about. "But then we should just probably, you know, forget it."

"Well, but no," said Stephanie, flipping another page. It said "The Iowa Connection" at the top, underlined twice. From farther back in the notebook she produced a printout of something: it was in color, and blurry. "When the camera shakes past the open door in *Targets*, you see this out in the yard."

Jeremy picked up the picture and looked at it. It was a corncrib, the old, short, squat kind you don't see much anymore. He'd played in them when he was a kid, but that felt like another world. He set it down decisively and pushed it back across the table.

"That's somewhere near here," she said. "It looks just like a lot of places near here."

"It looks like a lot of places anywhere," Jeremy said.

"No, they don't have corncribs everywhere."

"OK," Jeremy said. "But in Minnesota, Iowa, South Dakota. Missouri. Anywhere."

"It has to be here, though."

"No, it doesn't," Jeremy said, shaking his head a little. "It doesn't have to be anywhere. Look, I don't think I want to do this. I don't like this kind of thing. It's—"

He remembered lying in the dark in his room after watching *Targets*, unable to stop the scene he'd watched from replaying itself in his head. How it sped up and slowed down as his brain tried to find some context within which to situate it. The image seeking out and finding the internal circuits where it would be able to live forever. The figure under the canvas, rising. He remembered the feeling of worry, gnawing at him: real dread about the fate of the person who stood there, hooded, balancing on one foot.

"I don't like it," he said.

"How can you not be curious?" said Stephanie, irritated. She thumbed past a few more pages of printouts and stopped on a shot of the hooded woman. "This is somebody from around here."

Jeremy looked at it: the hood, the corner of the worktable, the pose.

"I guess maybe," he said. It felt good conceding her point, accepting as a possibility that there was a knowable explanation for the lonesome transferred scenes on the two tapes. Some way of understanding.

"Good," she said. "Here's what I've got." She turned the page again. There were new columns now: lists of people who lived on streets without names, rural routes or numbered highways. The whole county.

Jeremy averted his eyes, like he'd been exposed through no fault of his own to something obscene. "No," he said. "I'm not going out to Hubbard to knock on people's doors and look for a corncrib. No."

"Collins."

"Whatever."

"So why did you even meet with me?" she said. "If you don't care, why are we even talking?"

He got up to leave. "I only want to know because I can't help it," he said. "But I don't want to know anybody involved. I don't want to go to anybody's house and ask them questions."

She rose to follow him out. "We could just drive out there and look around."

"No," he said, opening the passenger door for her reflexively and shutting it after she got in, finishing his thought out loud as he walked around to the driver's side: "Be serious."

Back at the store Sarah Jane had locked the front door. Jeremy knocked, confused. It was the middle of the day.

"Somebody else complained about *She's All That*," she said after letting him in, "so I watched it." It was still playing on the in-store screen.

"I thought you already took it home."

"I did. But I didn't—I didn't watch it."

"Oh. Jeez," said Jeremy.

"You didn't tell me."

"I told you it freaked me out. I'm real sorry."

"No, it's OK," said Sarah Jane. "But what—" She reached for the remote and rewound to the spot.

It was the outbuilding. The door was open. When the camera jumped, Jeremy saw, clearly, because he was looking for it, the worktable. But that wasn't the focus of the scene, of course. The action in this one was under a tarp in the middle of the room. You couldn't say how many people were under it: maybe two, possibly three. Possibly only the one, the hooded figure from the chair. That was how Jeremy'd come to think of it, for his own sake: some idea of continuity made it easier.

But in fact you have to make a lot of assumptions to connect those earlier scenes to this one at any level deeper than their shared location. The figure or figures under the tarp buck and thrash, sometimes with a rolling movement, sometimes in violent jerks. You can hear breathing, and a sound that registers instantly as fingernails on canvas. With less than a minute left to go, the action steps up: a work boot at the end of a denim-clad leg enters the frame and prods a few times at the tarp, seeking a point of contact. A grasping hand shoots out from underneath, a flash of color; then the boot kicks the tarp three times, very deliberately. The kicks land with great thudding force. Someone underneath the tarp cries out incoherently, a frightened, choked stream of burbling vowels. Closer to the camera's mic, a man laughs and clears his throat.

Meanwhile, under the oilcloth, whoever's there is regrouping. Is it rising to its feet, singularly or collectively? Rolling over? Undergoing some sort of change in mass? No one can say. It's too dark to see much. Then *She's All That* blinks back, bright as day.

"Jeremy, what is this?" Sarah Jane said.

"I told you it freaked me out," said Jeremy.

"I can't have this in my store."

"Should we tell somebody?" He meant the police. It was the only idea he had.

"I guess maybe," said Sarah Jane, and she ejected the tape and put it back into its sleeve and headed back to the break room.

"We could just return it as defective," Jeremy said after her.

"Or that," she said over her shoulder, though in point of fact she neither called the police nor returned the tape to Northern Video, her distributor, for a replacement. Phone records and computer logs obtained from the Nevada Police Department show no calls or e-mails from Jeremy Heldt, Stephanie Parsons, or Sarah Jane Shepherd during this period. The Ames Police Department's records document several phone calls from Collins years later, of course, but by then new people were involved—strangers; variables from the cloudy distant future. The one thing you can never plan for, Mom used to say. Unexpected guests.

6 She wanted to throw it into the trash; she felt sick. It was disturbing to think that just last month, this thing had been sitting on her coffee table at home for several days, like a snake in a houseplant. It was hard to know where to start asking questions— who, what, why, where: the zeros in the timecode represented a whole separate set of *when* questions, off in their own universe of uncertainty. She looked the tape up in the system, thinking maybe she'd contact the distributor: *This is Sarah Jane Shepherd at Video Hut in Nevada. I think one of your suppliers* . . .

No. *This is Sarah Jane Shepherd at Video Hut in Nevada. Something's wrong with* . . .

No. *Hi, I got a tape from you that's had something else taped onto it and I think you should know about it*. Maybe. Transfer the responsibility. But they, in turn, bought their tapes from somebody else, and that's what they'd probably say: *Everything arrives at the Northern Video warehouse sealed. All we do is pick and pack. This is probably one of your customers.*

This is probably one of your customers. Video Hut did decent business, but was small. People who worked in Ames rented from Hollywood Video now. The customer base was shrinking. Stores like Sarah Jane's were on their way out: they'd served small towns since the dawn of the VCR boom, but they couldn't compete with volume. Count up the membership cards in the box on the counter by the computer terminal, throw out the ones that belonged to people who hadn't rented in over a year, and you'd know exactly how big the pool of possible suspects was.

So she took *She's All That* home with her that night, along with *Targets*—Jeremy'd called it "the other one, the old one"—and, from the comfort and safety of her recliner, fast-forwarded to the hard parts. Just like Stephanie Parsons, she took notes; but her own notes were very direct, item-by-item accounts of anything visible in the frame during the scenes in question, with no guesses or question marks. After running the *She's All That* scene twice, she reviewed her work while the movie played on. Working efficiently while a movie played was second nature to her by now, more comfortable than silence.

She was making a check mark by a line that said "cheap cardtable chair, something from a garage sale" when the end credits started. "Kiss Me" jangled along underneath while they rolled, warm and sentimental. Then, about halfway through, the song stopped, and the credits cut out, and the living room filled with light.

She left for Collins early the next morning, meaning to verify her suspicions and be back in time to open the store. She'd taken several Polaroids of the image on the screen during the end credits' most harrowing moment; a snapshot of a paused screen wasn't much, but you could still see the face clearly enough, the spatter drooling down its chin onto the dirt of the driveway. You could see the field off to the right. And you could see, finally, in the background, behind the woman apparently crawling away from it and toward the road, the unmistakable outline of a farmhouse; and you'd know, if you'd grown up anywhere nearby, exactly which house it was.

A woman in a faded floral-print dress, yellow daisies and blue cornflowers, answered the door. "Good morning," she said. "What can I do for you?"

Sarah Jane looked at her, trying not to stare too hard. "Sarah Jane Shepherd," she said; manners still came first. "My folks owned a farmhouse a little closer to town when I was a kid. I grew up over there."

"Well, good to meet you, Sarah Jane Shepherd," said the woman in the floral-print dress. "I'm Lisa. I came here about five years ago, I guess. I was up in Charles City before."

"Lisa—"

"Sample." She regarded Sarah Jane and extended her hand. "My folks were from Pottawattamie County."

"Near Grinnell?"

"No, that's Poweshiek." Sarah Jane nodded. "Pottawattamie's way over western Iowa. Almost Nebraska."

"Right, sure. Well—I was wondering if I could have a look at your outbuilding," said Sarah Jane, releasing Lisa's hand and gesturing across the driveway; she didn't see any point in putting it off. On the drive over she'd practiced a few reasons, and now she made her choice. "My dad wants to build himself a toolshed before summer." Her father had been dead for several years. It was a gamble.

Lisa came out through the screen door. Her feet were bare; there was some dirt underneath her toenails, enough to see it without needing a closer look. She looked to be in her early thirties, but her manner seemed older: she walked languidly, and spoke slowly, her voice deeper than the one Sarah Jane might have imagined coming from that young face.

"Sure—it's not much," she said, starting down the porch toward the building in question and beckoning Sarah Jane to follow her. "It was already on the property when I got here. I think it might be original with the house."

Inside the shed, its single overhead lightbulb too bright for the small space, Sarah Jane focused hard on her breathing, pretending to look into the corners she hadn't already seen on the tape. She paced the perimeter slowly, looking up to the ceiling and trying to think of questions. She hadn't thought far enough ahead.

"They don't make 'em like this anymore," she said after a while, pleased with herself.

"I guess not," said Lisa Sample. "Mainly people buy them pre-made now. No real reason to build one, I guess."

Sarah Jane thought very briefly about her life, about how little ever happened, and then she retrieved the printout of the paused frame from her purse. She didn't really believe she was about to show it to a total stranger, but she didn't see any other way to go about it.

"Listen," she said. "I saw a strange movie and I recognized the places in it from having grown up out this way. Look over here"—she jabbed at the right side of the page—"that's your house, right?"

Lisa leaned in to get a better look, then looked over at Sarah Jane. "I guess," she said. "Looks more or less like it. Pretty blurry."

"But this"—pointing now at the woman in the picture, her eyes a flash of panic in the grid—"this isn't you?"

Lisa laughed. "No, no," she said. She kept her eyes on the printout. "This must be from sometime before I got here."

The dot matrix wasn't great: if you didn't know what you were supposed to be looking at, you might have had trouble defining the features of the person pictured, the face in the grain. But

Sarah Jane had watched the sequence several times, concentrating hard. She'd traced the contours with her eyes and she knew what she was seeing now. She was sure of it.

They stood together there, in the place Sarah Jane knew beyond question was the set of the spliced-in scenes from the tapes, and nobody said anything for a minute.

"Huh," said Sarah Jane. "Well, I'm sorry to bother you."

"It's no bother," Lisa Sample said, reaching for the light switch as she headed back out toward the yard. "Can I get you a cup of coffee? There's coffee inside."

There is a variation on this story so pervasive that it's sometimes thought of not as a variation but as the central thread. In it, Sarah Jane returns to Video Hut a little after five, and describes for Jeremy much of what she saw in Collins. But she leaves out several important details: that the house in question is directly across the road from Bob Pietsch's place; that she stood waiting at the farmhouse's front door for several minutes before knocking on it; that the woman who answered was named Lisa, and that they'd spent much of the afternoon together in her living room. The story Sarah Jane brings home from Collins is deliberately incomplete, but she presents it with an air of totality, as if there were no more to say.

Jeremy's disappointed, but what can he do? He is out of ideas. Maybe the scenes on the tapes dry up, and in subsequent years he regards the entire episode as a momentary fancy, something he dreamed up because he was young and bored. This is the nail over which this particular variation's tires inevitably drive: Jeremy was young, but not so young. His mother's accident had taken care of that. And while his classmates from school had itched always for action, hitting the highway for Minneapolis or Chicago every weekend as soon as they could drive, he had stayed home. When he imagined himself all grown up, he saw himself in Nevada, maybe owning a store, or managing a business in Des Moines. If he thought of the future at all, it looked like the present. And so the young, bored Jeremy of the Nothing Happened variation rings false, and I put more stock in the one I see this afternoon, standing behind the counter eating a sandwich, reading through the classified ads in *The Des Moines Register*: the Jeremy who's there when Sarah Jane gets back from Collins, throwing herself wildly through the door of Video Hut as though seeking shelter, her eyes wide, her face darting deerlike first to the right, now to the left, the story she brings so fresh with the terror of its insult that she takes over an hour to tell it, like a person who's saying things out loud to make sure she won't forget them: a person testing the things in her mind against the hard surfaces of the world before venturing to claim that yes, they're true and real, and have form, and shape, and weight, and meaning.

7   "The hood—it was right there on the chair—not the chair, a real chair, an old one, big wooden one—right there, right there in the hallway."

"I—"

"She asked me in"—here extending her hand, *water, anything,* Jeremy looking around, finally grabbing the thirty-two-ounce Coke he'd brought back from Dairy Queen with lunch and handing it to her—"and the house looked normal, she's normal, but all the things, they're right there—" and here, putting her palm to her face, testing it with her fingers. She had a scratch on her cheek, a round-ish abraded blotch.

"Slow down," Jeremy said. His mother'd said that to him when he'd had bad dreams as a child. *Slow down. Tell me about it.*

"I went to the house," she said.

"The house?"

"It was right there."

"Slow down."

"Those scenes on the tapes, the ones you said."

"What house."

"You can see a house. It's not there for long but you can see it, I saw it. It clicked right away. I—"

"Slow down."

"When she's getting up, in the one scene." She extended her arms, mimicking the hooded figure's rise to her feet. "In the other one, too. If you freeze the tape, there's a house. I froze the tape. I grew up out there. I know that house."

She drew soda up through the straw in huge gulps.

"I grew up out there," she said again. She looked at Jeremy, making sure he was there to bear witness. "That place has been there since I was a kid."

"Collins?" said Jeremy.

"The *house*," said Sarah Jane, reaching back into her purse and retrieving the printout of the frame from when my hand slipped and the front porch came into view.

A farmhouse has a way of feeling both timeless and impermanent without ever committing to either side. Seen from the road, buttressed by its fields, it bequeaths order to the frame: those fields, now that a farmhouse sits squarely in their midst, are there for someone. They're justified. Inside—in the narrow entry hall; in the kitchen opening onto the living room; upstairs—there's a lived-in feel; the house is there for the fields outside its windows. Coffee cans on pantry shelves, clean dishtowels embroidered with roosters or the sun and smartly draped over the handle of the stove—when, here, did people not live like this?

But a farmhouse has no neighbors, not real ones, and if you try looking for them, it shrinks. Its architecture is functional, its staircase carpeted old pine, not oak or maple; its window frames were painted white once long ago and never touched up again. Walk twenty paces from its door and you're waist-high in corn or knee-high in bean fields, already forgetting the feel of being behind a door, safely shielded from the sky.

Whether you're inside or out walking rows, though, you're invisible. If we talk about seeing the house from the road, "in passing" is implied. No one inventories the shelves or the drawers or pulls up the staircase carpet, worn down from years of use. The only people likely to take much note of a farmhouse are the ones who go there on purpose: to get something, or to bring news, or because they live there.

"No," Jeremy said when Sarah Jane finished.

"Please," she said. "I don't want to go back there alone."

"I'm not going. Why do you—" Jeremy started, cutting himself off before saying *you two. Why do you two want to go out there.*

"I want to know," said Sarah Jane after a little silence, knowing Jeremy, even in defiance, was too polite to ask *Know what?* She reached into her purse and retrieved her printout, now half-crumpled in one corner.

Jeremy appraised it. "I never saw this one," he said.

"It's after the credits." Specifically, it was after someone had turned on the floodlights in the driveway; the action washes out to a pure white throughout the scene, swallowed by an incoming tide of light and then reemerging. "She tries to get away, I thought. But it's her."

Jeremy took in the picture as best he could; the unhooded figure was in disarray, only half-clothed now. Looking at it made him feel ashamed of something, he wasn't sure what.

"Her?"

"The woman who lives in the house now. Lisa. She said it wasn't but I know it is."

"This is something we should just leave alone," said Jeremy, surprised to hear himself sounding so assertive. But it was true: this had all gone far enough for him.

"I have to go back," said Sarah Jane, without enthusiasm, as if describing an unpleasant duty.

"OK," said Jeremy, unsure how to understand the way it seemed as if she were asking his permission. Her visible distress made him uncomfortable; he wanted to do or say whatever he could to calm her down, but without having to learn much more about the source of her discomfort.

"I have to go back," she said again as she began straightening up the front counter a little: just keeping her hands busy, easing unsurely back into the normal quiet of the day.

Ezra was there when Jeremy came in for the afternoon shift the next day: his car, an old Chevrolet Citation with black-orange rust moons pocking its rims, stood blue and alone in the parking lot, a little worse off for having survived another winter. Their paths didn't cross often; Ezra mainly worked the evening rush on weekends. Still, they greeted each other with nods and grunts, like men who'd seen each other every morning at the grain elevator for years.

"Sarah Jane sick?" Jeremy asked with his back turned while hanging up his coat.

"I guess sick," Ezra said. "She called me last night and asked if I could pick up her shift. Said the key was under the mat."

"The mat at her house?"

"No, the one out front." Jeremy raised his eyebrows. The mat out front would be swollen with rain and melting snow until at least May, but putting the key to the store there seemed crazy.

"Huh," said Jeremy.

The store was clean and there weren't any returns to file; there would be nothing to do until the after-work rush. They waited out the quiet until the rush did come, then worked briskly until it died down. Jeremy was talking to Bob Pietsch about smallmouth bass in the Dale Maffitt Reservoir this year when the phone rang. "You have to be a little patient," Bob was saying when Ezra picked it up.

"I don't like to go out this early," said Jeremy. "Might as well go up north and do it on the ice. Save the local spots for summer."

"Fished all winter down here growing up, though."

"Sure," said Jeremy.

"She asked if I could pick up the rest of her shifts this week," Ezra said when he'd gotten off the phone. Through the window, you could see the blast of steam and exhaust from Bob's pickup as he pulled out onto the road.

"Mm," said Jeremy. "Flu?"

"She didn't say. She just said she wasn't coming in."

"Well, it's her store."

"It's her store," Ezra agreed. Neither man could really imagine many situations that would cause a person to call off work for a whole week. Even out-of-town funerals only took a day or two. They finished out the shift without saying any more about it, and nodded goodbyes in the parking lot.

"I'll see you tomorrow, I guess," Ezra said.

"Yeah, I'll see you then," said Jeremy, trying, as he turned the key in the ignition, to shake off the urge to drive out to Collins instead of heading home.

He drove past the highway on-ramp steadily. His imagination flared with the variables—smoke, fire, fumes—but he shook his head a couple of times to get his head clear, and it worked. You cultivate practical responses all your life precisely so that you'll instinctively protect yourself if you should happen to meet a moment like this one, where, nagged by worry, you find yourself tempted to get on a dark highway at night and see who is or isn't parked down a farmhouse driveway. You hold out for a better scenario: the next morning, say, when it's light out, and the moon isn't up. You hold out for the right time so as not to make things worse.

But the situation as it eventually revealed itself to him in the house did not align with his expectations, though it was elliptically consonant with what he'd pictured. Bracing yourself against the possibility of disaster came naturally to him; it seemed to run in the family, and in the families of most people he knew. Plan for colder winters, harder storms, road closures. In the unmanageable elements of the case before him, though, expectations had been lowered to the point of paranoia: he saw himself arriving at the property in Collins and walking unprotected into scenes of unspeakable devastation and loss, too late to help anyone, too much gone for any explanation-offering reassembly to ever be attempted.

As we know, the Collins house played a longer game. But the memory of his first vision proved hard to shake. And indeed, all the way down to the present day, Jeremy will sometimes find himself replaying the payoff he'd first imagined, that vivid, unrealized presentiment: of taking matters into his own hands and turning the CLOSED sign around before sundown. Driving to Collins. Heading down a gravel road, a cloud of dust rising from his back tires as he sped toward the titanic orange beacon of Lisa Sample's house, now in flames, oil-black smoke ascending into the Iowa sky in a single furious spiraling column, the sound of the fire reaching him before he was physically near enough to hear it, the rumble and the roar.

8   The drive in from Collins took half an hour. She'd hoped to get to the store in time to open it herself; there'd be no chance of avoiding some kind of confrontation, she knew, but getting there first might establish a power dynamic, some system of domain: just being inside already when Jeremy reported for work, sitting behind the counter, scrolling through the overdues.

But she got caught behind a combine harvester on the surface streets out to 65 North, and it set her back a full fifteen minutes. Jeremy was already inside. She tried not to be nervous—they'd talked at least once a day on the phone—but there was no way he wasn't going to ask, and she still hadn't settled on an answer.

She fired the first volley as she came in through the door. "Everything all right?" she said.

Jeremy laughed. "Nobody's been in yet," he said. "Everything's like usual. Are you in today?"

"I think so," she said, her strategy presenting itself to her in the moment, naturally, like magic. "Haven't been able to keep any food down. I'll spare you the details. Just got a full breakfast down for the first time in days, anyway."

Jeremy thought about his dad, about the partial conversations they'd been having at the dinner table the past two weeks, ever since Sarah Jane had stopped coming in; and thought also about the bigger picture he'd been trying to bring into focus, the story. What did his father think? His father thought the whole deal was a little weird, but probably nothing to worry about. "People can have things going on in their private lives," he'd said one night over some pot roast. "You never really know. If it's me, I just take the extra hours."

"Gets pretty quiet when you're putting in forty hours at Video Hut," Jeremy'd said.

"I can imagine." He'd helped himself to some more mashed potatoes. You think you'd get tired of them, but it takes longer than you'd think. "Did I mention how Bill Veatch is looking for help? Just if you wanted to get your hands a little dirtier, I guess. Needs somebody in receiving."

"Full-time?"

"I think," his father'd said. "Give him a call."

But Jeremy wasn't ready to call Bill Veatch yet. First he wanted to know why Sarah Jane wasn't coming in to the store anymore; why she'd put him on opening duty almost daily for two straight weeks. Why Ezra had to pick up so many hours all of a sudden. Ezra didn't usually get this much contact with the outside world; it made Jeremy feel obligated to protect him. On duty, they hardly ever exchanged more than a few sentences, but the governing silence between them was the regional grammar of comfort between like-minded men. They enjoyed each other's company. Still, Jeremy thought kids like Ezra shouldn't have to come all the way into town every day. It messed with the order of things.

"So just a flu bug or something?" he said, back in the present, in the incoming glare of the morning.

"I wonder," she said, improvising now, enjoying it. "I remember my mom used to have all kinds of trouble after she started getting older."

It was a powerful gambit. Talking about family health is a pastime almost as exalted as the noble art of who lives where now and how they got there. The cue was right there waiting for him to pick it up, if he wanted to: grandmothers, aunts, cousins. The path of no resistance was open. But he wanted to know, so he pressed forward.

"Have you been to a doctor?" he asked.

She was back in the racks pulling tapes; she hadn't bothered to retrieve the outer sleeves from the aisles. Her fingers flipped at the corners of the clear cases like a chicken's beak picking up seed. She was hunting down specific titles. It seemed pretty clear.

"I have an appointment," she said.

"You want a bag for those?" Jeremy offered, reaching under the counter and rustling among the plastic Hy-Vee bags.

"I'll just take them to the car," she said, offhandedly, automatically but with a weirdly cheerful air; she had five tapes in all. Jeremy watched her head out to the parking lot; she popped the trunk and set them down inside, quite carefully, it seemed, as you might with something fragile.

"Been all holed up in the house, haven't really seen anybody for a while," she said when she came back in. "Do I look awful?"

"You look about the same to me," said Jeremy, which wasn't true at all.

"Well, it's sweet of you to say that," she said, reaching into her jeans for some Chap Stick, applying it to her lips like it was the most normal thing in the world, her lips in fact dry and cracked and peeling, her eyes weirdly awake to the fluorescent hum of the almost-empty store.

"Which ones did she take?" Stephanie asked on the phone.

"Miss Parsons, I don't get into anybody's business," Jeremy said. Why had he called her, then?

"Why did you call me, then?" she said.

"Well, you asked how she was last time you were in."

"It could have waited if that was all there was to it."

"Well, I'm sorry, then," said Jeremy.

"Don't get mad," she said. "I just don't know why you won't admit to being a little curious."

"You already made me admit that," he said.

Stephanie smiled. Jeremy's shyness was the true vintage.

"Go see which tapes," she said.

He didn't feel like arguing; it's easier to follow directions. He got up from the stool behind the counter and went back into the racks. The store was already locked; Sarah Jane had said she'd be back after lunch, but an hour later the phone rang. The doctor wanted her to get more rest. She was going home. "You want somebody to bring you some dinner?" he'd asked her.

"No, no," she'd said.

"Looks like those two we saw, you and me," Jeremy said now to Stephanie, "plus *Iron Will*, and one called *Primal Fear*. And a *Star Trek* movie."

"Which *Star Trek*?"

He laughed. "I don't know." He walked with the mobile phone to his ear from the racks out into the store again and headed for the Sci-Fi section. He grabbed four of the *Star Trek* titles and headed back to the racks again.

"OK, we still have *Generations*," he said. "Still have *Insurrection*. We're missing *First Contact*, it looks like."

"The case is in the store and the tape's gone?" said Stephanie.

"Yeah." He imagined her scribbling in her notebook full of lists and heavily underlined phrases in capital letters.

"We should get that one from Hollywood Video and watch it," she said.

"I'm not doing this with you," he said. "I'm just telling you because I knew you'd want to know."

There was a pause. "Do you have a crush on me?" she said.

"Sure," he said. "A little. I don't know."

She didn't want to push him, in part because she sensed that pushing would be of no use, but she'd outgrown the patience for these slow, shy passes.

"Well, I'm going into Ames, and I'm going to Hollywood Video," she said.

"All right," he said. "Let me know if you find anything, I guess." She wasn't going to find anything. Sarah Jane had the only copy on which anybody might have found something. If Stephanie didn't already know this, then she was just playing games.

"I'll call you after I watch," she said, and she did, that night, around 11:30; they talked for about fifteen minutes, maybe twenty, about *Star Trek: First Contact*, and also about recent trends in the weather.

Hanging from a nail at the end of the front porch was a hollowed-out gourd with a hole in it for birds. House wrens will set up shop in a gourd inside of half a day if you hang one up; they nest in winter and their young fledge in spring, and then the nest sits ready for another bird to come clear it out and start again.

"Wasps," Lisa Sample said from her chair near the door when

she saw Sarah Jane approaching the gourd. "They'll come at you if you hang out over there too much."

"Sorry?"

"Wasps. There used to be birds, but between nests some wasps set up in there. We had them when I lived in Madison. Look." She pointed at the hole; it was partially obscured by a pale tan resin, leaving a half-moon-shaped opening. "Brood cells."

Sarah Jane jutted her neck forward a little and narrowed her eyes, trying to get better focus without having to draw nearer; she noticed a few small yellow bodies lazily drifting in and out of the hole. It made the gourd feel heavier in her sight than it had when she'd been imagining robins or nuthatches. Birds nest lightly. She thought about so many wasps crowded into one place, a great throng displacing some small family of two or three birds. She saw the muddy netting of the nest half-blocking the hole, dusty runover from all the activity inside. And she noted, finally, a wet spot at the bottom, a darkening patch about as big as her hand. Honey? There is no wasp honey. But the gourd had been put there for birds.

"Madison?" she said.

"Just for a short while. It was nice, though," said Lisa, behind her now, craning in, voice low. "I think they got one of the babies before the mama left. Gourd'll rot through when it gets a little warmer now."

"They eat birds?" said Sarah Jane. Her stomach heaved a little.

"They eat mosquitoes. They'll sting anything, though. I guess if something happened to a little bird in there the mama wouldn't really be able to pull it back out through the little hole."

"That's terrible," Sarah Jane almost said, but she stopped herself, because she wasn't sure it was what she meant. Maybe it's terrible, the dead bird inside the gourd, the gourd full of wasps hanging from the rail on the porch, the wet spot spreading on the bottom of the gourd. But maybe there was a better explanation for the spot, something about dewpoints and organic matter and the lifespan of an empty gourd. Nothing was really certain. She reached into her purse.

"I brought two. I didn't want to answer a bunch of questions," she said instead, handing Lisa the tapes, their bulky cases dully reflecting a little sun. She heard the hum inside the gourd grow a little louder and dutifully took a step back.

"They will swarm," said Lisa, turning discreetly, tapes in hand. Sarah Jane followed her inside; they stood behind the screen door, watching as a few wasps ventured out to see if the shadows they'd felt required a response. "I've had to run inside real quick a couple of times."

"Couldn't you call Orkin and just get rid of them?" asked Sarah Jane.

But Lisa had a dreamy look on her face; the sentry wasps were tracing patterns in the sunlight. "I guess," she said quietly, still under the spell of the lazy figure eights the wasps followed in the air. "But it seems kind of mean. It's their home now, you know?"

She closed the door and turned, heading for the cellar steps. "It's just nature," she said conclusively, but also, as it seemed to Sarah Jane, sadly, as if somewhere in the question of the birds and the wasps there was something to be regretted, but nowhere that any reasonable person might fix the blame.

9 "Hello?"

"Big man? It's Dad."

"Hi."

"Hi. I just thought I'd call and see if—hey, listen. I was thinking about getting dinner in Des Moines." A beat. "There's a friend from work, we thought we might get dinner together."

Steve listened to the short silence after he'd said it; it was a rift in something. Jeremy felt it too. They almost always had dinner together. It gave shape to their days.

"Oh, OK," said Jeremy.

"If you'd rather I—" Steve looked at the wall of his office; he was calling from work. Next to an old family portrait on the wall above the desk, there was a printout of a *Love is . . .* cartoon. *Love is . . . the greatest feeling you can feel!* It had been there for years; it came from another time.

"No, it's no problem, Dad. I'll fix myself something. See you later?"

"I won't be late," said Steve. "See you later, then."

"Sure," said Jeremy. It was true. He wasn't going anywhere.

"If you're up later, let's visit a little," his father said finally, trying to hide the effort it took to say it under the easy burble he used when talking to clients.

"All right," said Jeremy.

He was at the Spaghetti Works in Des Moines. Sitting across the table from him, eating a piece of garlic bread, was Shauna Kinzer; she was an office manager at a lumberyard. He'd been nodding casual hellos to her for several years; a couple of times they'd had lunch, nothing fancy, just an Applebee's out near a site they were both involved with. In the middle of fine-tuning the details on a big job, he'd asked if she'd like to get dinner, and she'd given him an easy, natural yes that filled him with a quiet warmth. He'd been nervous, worried that she could see it. It had been a long time. She'd ordered the pepperoni chicken.

"Chicken all right?" he said.

"It's great," she said, smiling at him. "I always try to order something I wouldn't make for myself at home."

Steve twirled his spaghetti against a spoon and gave a small laugh. "My house has two grown men in it," he said. "We eat a lot of spaghetti."

"Are you the cook?"

"We take turns," he said. "If you brown your own beef you can make a pretty nice sauce. We get kind of competitive."

It seemed early, but she saw an opening, and she liked him. "How long have you two—" Not quite. "When was—"

"Winter of ninety-four." He stabbed and twirled. There was a small beat; kitchen sounds, other tables talking, laughing at something. "Christmastime."

"I can't imagine."

Steve chewed his food for a minute, and swallowed, giving the moment the time it needed. "It's all right now. Thanks, though. Honestly," he said, and he meant it. From early on he'd had to hear lots of people tell him how Linda was in a better place now. Right out of the gate: *She's in a better place now.* Why did they say that?

"How old—"

"Jeremy," he said. "Sixteen. That's really the hardest part, you know. You don't know what to say. To him. To anybody, I guess, but . . . it was hard."

"I am so sorry, Steve."

"It's all right," he said. "We miss her, you know. But we know she'd want us to be strong, that's what she would have wanted. I wish she could see our boy, you know. He—he's a good boy," he said, his voice breaking a little, because he hardly ever talked about it; he was surprised to find himself feeling so open.

"Good kid, I mean," he said, clearing his throat, taking a drink of water. Jeremy hadn't been a boy for many years. "He's always been a good kid."

"He is lucky to have a good dad," Shauna Kinzer said very deliberately, reaching across the table and putting her hand on his. The warmth soaked into his skin, rain on cracked earth.

They ordered dessert: two hot fudge brownies; sharing just one would have felt awkward. Out in front of the restaurant they said their good nights and then drove off in separate cars.

Ken Wahl, M.S.W., M.F.C.C.: 15 years experience in central Iowa. Individual and couples counseling. Specializing in grief, loss, and transition—it had been the least flowery ad in the Des Moines Yellow Pages back in 1995; it was important to Steve that the people he chose to share his private troubles with weren't the type to try to convince him to cry out loud, and that they lived at least one county away.

Ken Wahl saw Steve Heldt clearly; over the years he'd known lots of men who didn't want to make spectacles of themselves, whose need to retain their composure often surpassed their desire to be healed. "Did you ever think about keeping a journal?" he'd asked casually during their second meeting, and Steve had said no, he'd never been much on writing: but Wahl had reached into a big drawer in his desk and pulled out a composition book.

"You might try to write a little in it every day," he said. "Just to see if it helps. You don't have to show it to anybody, not even me, unless you feel like it—we can do that, but we don't have to. It's not for reading. Some people just find it comforting to write all this stuff down."

You or I, finding ourselves in Steve Heldt's shoes, might fill this book with intricate reckonings of our grief, trying to empty ourselves of its burden. But Steve only ever finished a few entries, which he meant to share with Wahl, but never did. The first few pages were simple sleep diaries: *Two hours, 11:00–1:00; awake, watched TV until 5:00, fell asleep on couch.* He'd ventured a little inward later, remembering all the times he thought of Linda during a given day: at work, while driving, before bed. At lunch with a client, having to swallow it all down. And then, suddenly: this.

Some accounts of Steve Heldt's journal omit this entry, while other versions of his story make no mention of any diary at all. I place full credence in both the journal and its disputed, penulti-mate entry, which feels true, like a purge. A years-long gap followed in its wake: this, too, makes sense to me. Steve began journaling with a view toward completing an unpleasant task, and when he thought the job was done, he stopped.

I wonder if I can really tell you what it was like to lose Linda, how heavy the blow was to me. She was the mother of my only son; that's not even what I really mean, when I hear it out loud like this, because he's not my son, he's our son. In February 1978 I drove her to Mary Greeley during a snowstorm in the middle of the night, because the contractions were coming too fast for us to wait any longer; she was sailing through early labor really fast, and we were young and scared, and I didn't know what would happen, but I tried to stay strong, because I thought that was what she needed, and I always try to stay level-headed in choppy waters: that's what I'm good at, it's one of the things people know me by. Good old Steve, never flies off the handle. But I couldn't stop my mind from scaring up all these worst-case scenarios, things I was afraid of: complications, terrifying grisly scenes. In my daily life, at work, at home, I don't dwell on possible bad outcomes. What's the point? If anything worries me I swat away the worry like a bug, but on the drive to the hospital it was like waves of worry crashing inside me. I focused on the road and told Linda just to keep breathing, that it wouldn't be long.

That was the night our son was born! Men cry all the time now, it seems like, over any old thing, but it wasn't like that then, and anyway, I'm not ashamed to admit I cried. Our son was so beautiful. He was perfect. A round little baby boy. Linda was tired afterward, so tired, and she and Jeremy both slept almost constantly for the next three days, and again I started worrying: that something might be wrong, that it wasn't normal for him to sleep so much, that we ought to call the doctor. But she comforted me, and she said in that quiet, whispery voice: Steve, it's OK. That's what she was like. Even in her own exhaustion she helped me stay the course. All this is normal, she told me, that little baby so sweet, sound asleep on her chest and the house so quiet, and then as the ship steadied itself we began to grow into the family we became, a happy family for sixteen whole years. His first day of school. Christmases. Summer vacations.

You don't think about how you really have your whole life planned out until a part of it goes missing suddenly one day. You'll panic then. I don't care who you are. But for Jeremy's sake and to make Linda proud I kept myself sane, and we got through it.

I'll always miss Linda and I know Jeremy does, too, but he almost never talks about her, and I don't know what I should do. I can't tell if he needs help, if there's something special a father's supposed to do for his son when they're in a situation like ours. I'm a guy who works on projects with blueprints, but I'm on my own here. It feels dark a lot of the time; I thought it would clear up, and it's eased a little, but it's still dark. So I watch what's left of my life like a security guard on the night shift, checking the locks when I know I don't need to, pacing the perimeter of someplace nobody's going to break into, except that you never know. Something could happen. So you keep watch. They don't pay security guards just because they're a few bodies short on the payroll.

He drove home up Interstate 35, the sky so dark, the air cold. Reading the highway signs for Saylorville Lake he got that sentimental urge some men get to spend a day fishing with their sons. It seemed like a good opening. When he got home and found Jeremy in the living room watching the highlight reel, he tried it out: "Passed Saylorville Lake on the way home," he said.

"Yeah? Bob Pietsch says he had to throw back more bluegill than he could take home last time he went out," Jeremy said.

"We should get out there sometime," Steve offered, pleased with himself: no false notes in the opening. They were talking like guys at work.

"Sure," said Jeremy.

Steve kept his eye on the TV as he spoke. "Had dinner with Shauna Kinzer," he said. "Did I tell you about Shauna Kinzer?"

Jeremy looked at his dad over there on the other end of the

couch, the screenlight flickering on his face. "I don't think so," he said.

"Well, she's somebody I met at a job site." Baylor was beating the Cyclones again. "We kept running into each other and then tonight we got supper together. It was kind of a date."

State couldn't seem to do anything against ranked opponents this year. Jeremy wanted to tell his dad it was all right if he went out on a date, but he wasn't sure if he meant it or if it just felt like the right thing to say, so he waited.

"We had a good time. She's a really nice person. It's nice to have somebody to talk to. I'd like to ask her out again."

"You shouldn't feel bad if you want to spend time with somebody, Dad," said Jeremy, very tenderly, trying to help. "Like, go on dates. I mean, it's fine. It's great. But you don't have to ask my permission. Or my blessing, I don't know. It's *all right*."

Steve regarded his son for a second. All grown up. He wondered what somebody else in his shoes might have done, but he couldn't think of many similar cases. Bob Pietsch, maybe. Maybe not. "I know I don't," he said then. "It just feels a little strange. I thought we should might have a little talk about it, I guess. I don't know."

There was a space of a few breaths. Steve looked up at the shelf by the sliding glass door that led to the backyard: there was a framed family portrait from Oceans of Fun, back when Jeremy was in grade school.

"It's always going to feel strange without Mom," Jeremy said.

"Do you think—do you think it'd be all right with your mom?" Steve said, miles high in the darkness now, airless, trying to acclimate himself to the cold.

"Well, sure," said Jeremy. "I mean, sure. She'd want you to meet somebody, I mean. She was like that."

It was true. It was one of the things Steve missed most. Linda

58

knew what was best for him, and whatever was best for him was what she wanted, too; she'd always seemed happiest if she could put him at ease. There are people who talk to their loved ones in prayer, who seek guidance and hear something in the gap between asking and the subsequent silence, but Steve Heldt had never been one of those people. Linda was buried in Nevada Municipal Cemetery. He was certain of it. He had seen her lowered into the grave.

"I want to do right by your mother," Steve said.

Baylor scored again. Jeremy wished his mom could send some sign to Dad from somewhere: from the stars, from a dream, from down in the soil.

"You should be happy in your life, Dad," said Jeremy. They left it there.

In the darkness of his room, after the game, Jeremy lay awake trying to get angry about the Cyclones not being any good this year. But in his heart he didn't care about the Cyclones, not like he had in the past. His heart was elsewhere now, and what he really wanted to think about was Bill Veatch and that opening in receiving, what all that might look like. Bill'd pay better than Sarah Jane, there wasn't any doubt about that; there'd be opportunities for advancement, too. Veatch & Son had offices in Des Moines and Cedar Rapids, big operations. Anything involved with construction was going to be solid for a while. Out in Ames near the North Grand Mall they had whole new neighborhoods going up. Who knew where any of the people living in them were supposed to find work—maybe they were mainly students? How did their parents afford these places?—but somebody had to be buying those houses, and somebody had to build them.

Jeremy didn't see himself like those people who just drift from job to job: friends from high school tending bar in Campustown, staying up late with the waitresses. Morning shift clerks at Kum & Go. But signing on with a growing business—he felt pretty sure Bill Veatch would hire him more or less on sight—that was a commitment. Stephanie Parsons had talked about teaching abroad once, but that wasn't right either. Not everybody wants to get out and see the world. Nothing wrong with that. Sometimes you just want to figure out how to fit yourself into the world you already know.

Besides: there was Dad. Jeremy felt like it was time to make room for his father. It was a strange feeling, thinking about Dad like this, as a person whose life might be distinct from his own. The two of them had shaped the space they lived in around his mother's absence; they'd made it a comfortable place you didn't have to think about too much. It was a known quantity, a knowable outcome. In local terms, that was its strength, but some nights at dinner Jeremy looked at his father and felt a sadness he couldn't quite name.

What if he just got out of the way? It would be strange. He'd get used to it. They'd both get used to it. Maybe it would be for the best.

He didn't resolve anything just yet, but he registered the presence of some slow movement inside himself, a small change in the coordinates of his inner drift. He rolled over from his back onto his side. The last thing he saw before he fell asleep was the glint of a baseball trophy he'd gotten in fourth grade, still sitting on the same shelf where he'd put it all those years ago. His team had finished fourth overall. Everybody got a trophy. It was a statue of a player with a bat in his hands, waiting for the pitch.

10 It happened in a haze: one minute the car was carrying her through the dark down the road from Collins, stars and moon overhead, no light due for at least an hour, and the next she was riding back out, the car a little emptier but not palpably so, divested of its burden. She hardly ever drove into Nevada anymore: maybe to run payroll, or to show her face at the counter long enough to keep people from asking questions. Of the actual errand she could later recall only tangential details—her reflection in the glass door as she approached it in the glare of a streetlight; the extra minute she had to wait on the way back out for the early morning traffic to pass before she could turn left onto Lincoln Way.

It was sloppy, that huge pile of tapes all at once on the floor. How is something like that not a cry for help? Someone working with footage from a camera mounted on her rearview, monitoring her face as she drove, might have tried, in edit, to frame the scene like that—as Sarah Jane reaching out somehow, trying to get caught. This is a mood I can imagine if all this had taken place in South Carolina, maybe: all that salty air, high humidity, the coast giving way to broken shoreline. Or New Mexico, up in the mountains. The New Mexico Sarah Jane I can envision letting some anxiety bleed right through her expression, steering through the switch-backs on the way up to her cabin.

But the Iowa Sarah Jane, the real one, has no beads of sweat forming on her forehead. Her jaw doesn't tremble and her hands don't shake. The several rings she wears on her fingers click a little against the steering wheel, keeping time with a melody only she can hear, but she is otherwise indistinguishable from anyone else driving down the same road. She'd gone in early because Lisa Sample had knocked in the middle of the night and told her it was time. Time for what? Time to take the tapes back. Take them back? Yes, they're finished, they should go back out on the shelves, I can only hold on to them for so long. All right, but all at once? Yes, I think so: who'll know, besides you and me? They'll only get out a little at a time: this with that smile, that hybrid of kindness and hunger she'd never seen anywhere else.

You'd expect, in the presence of any inner struggle, to see it re-flected here, in the privacy of the highway, where no one is watching. But that after-midnight conversation, and any news it brought about the nature of Lisa's work, has gone away to hide in the place where all the other moments they share end up: in a secret cham-ber of Sarah Jane's heart, where the person she'd hoped to be by now has set up shop and is making do with available materials.

So think instead of animals that shed skins. It's a metaphor with limited uses: there aren't any animals in play here. Everybody's a free agent. Still, picture the noble snake, having molted, slither-ing away, newly glistening. There's the skin, in a big disorganized pile behind it. Is the snake asking you to notice that a snake was here earlier? No; the snake doesn't care one way or the other. It has moved on. No, indeed, you can't call a snake sloppy or careless or fault it for leaving tracks in its wake. Besides, who are you? Snakes have been here for millions of years.

There was a small mountain of tapes on the other side of the door when Jeremy opened the store the next morning. The overnight return didn't normally get a lot of use; there was an extra heft to the door as he pushed it open. He deactivated the alarm first and then started moving tapes from the floor to the counter. It took a while.

The unexpected stack of returns threw off his routine; he forgot to put a tape into the player for in-store play. Instead he sat at the counter, processing returns in silence, pronouncing titles in his head as he checked them all back in: *Tango & Cash*, *Varsity Blues*, *Primal Fear*, *She's All That*, *Mortal Thoughts*, *Bloodsport*, *Targets*, *Nightbreed*, *Reindeer Games*, *The Sweet Hereafter*, *Trading Mom*, *Universal Soldier*, *Shadowlands*. He was running an internal inventory of which ones he had and hadn't seen when Stephanie came in. "Hi, stranger," she said.

"Hello stranger yourself," said Jeremy. Their meeting at Gregory's was comfortably tucked away behind the last long freeze that preceded the spring thaw; it was May now. He was happy to see her.

"Keeping busy?"

"Sure," he said. "I'm kind of the acting manager these days. How're you?"

"I'm looking at a job in San Francisco," she said, trying casually to slide "San Francisco" onto the end of the phrase like you might say "Clive" or "Colo" or "Marshalltown." "You think they have a Video Hut there?"

"Management opportunities at Blockbuster," said Jeremy. Their smiles sparked off each other in the same instant. Stephanie thought about how bored she'd been all winter.

She grabbed a movie from the racks without really looking at it and put it on the counter. "I'm going," she said.

"I believe you." He rang her up and handed her the tape. *Excalibur.*

"You should go someplace, too, Jeremy," she said.

"Well, and I might someday."

"Seriously. You have to get out of Iowa."

He wrinkled his brow, alone there in the store with Stephanie, trying not to feel stung but thinking she could probably see it on him.

"No, I don't," he said.

"You're right," she said, their eyes meeting. Not too long. "I hope I see you before I leave, anyway." Then she smiled the smile that few outside the region will ever master, a no-problems look that paves over rough road without making any big deal about it. But he felt the needle land where she'd aimed it, as he did sometimes when people who didn't understand his family weighed in about his life, telling him how it looked from the outside. Another nagging little question lodged like a bit of grapeshot in his chest. It was nothing major, but the place where he stored them all was running out of room.

He called Bill Veatch from work, muting the in-store TV before he did it. It'd been a slow day in the store; it seemed like it was all slow days now. Bill himself answered, but only to say he wasn't much good at talking on the phone: could Jeremy come in tomorrow? Sure, he had tomorrow off, tomorrow morning would be fine.

The Veatch & Son offices in Des Moines took up a full city block just off I-35. Thom Veatch, with a government loan, had founded Veatch Basement & Foundation after coming home from the Second World War, where he'd served in the Pacific theater; over the next ten years industrial growth around town slowed to a trickle, but he'd already been able to open offices in Sioux City and Council Bluffs by then. His main line of work was waterproofing; one of his salesmen, a real carny barker type, had a line about how you needed to waterproof your basement on both sides of the boom-and-bust cycle. It was true. Applying sealant to baseboards and cinder blocks wasn't the kind of work people aspired to, but there'd always be the work to do, and if on top of that you were the man who sold the cinder blocks, so much the better.

By the time Thom Veatch died in 1987, he had five locations throughout the state, and had expanded his home office's operations to include building materials—wood, concrete—and machine rental. He left the whole business to his son William, who'd graduated from the College of Business and Public Administration at Drake. There were actually two Veatch sons, but Bill's brother, Gary, had driven a VW van out to Oregon immediately after high school and didn't want anything to do with construction. So it was just Veatch & Son.

Bill was in his late forties now; it seemed like there was a new Home Depot going up somewhere in Polk County every week. Young men ran into the Home Depot recruiter at the job fair and ended up replacing PVC under residential sinks all day, but Bill wasn't going down without a fight. He liked the Iowa he'd grown up in and wanted to leave something of it to his own kids if he could.

It was the third job interview Jeremy'd ever done; he'd gotten a harvest help job at the co-op when he was sixteen without even filling out an application first. With Sarah Jane it'd been more of a conversation than an interview; she talked about starting Video Hut after her divorce, figuring out the mechanics of the business all by herself, learning how to stand on her own two feet. But Bill Veatch spoke in broad terms, and his outlook grew more appealing as he went, taking on softly cinematic properties in Jeremy's imagination.

A reliable day's work; a few bills in his pocket; money in the bank. Making the drive out daily from Nevada until maybe he met someone. A family? Move closer to work, then, probably. Or possibly not; there was nothing wrong with commuting to work. All kinds of people did it. He'd seen a bunch of them behind the wheels of their cars on the highway just this morning, cups of coffee in one hand and the other on the wheel. It was something of a perk, according to Bill: "House fills up with kids, you love 'em, but half an hour on the highway, it's like a little vacation," he said when they'd reached the far fence, from which you could see the cars up on I-35. "Sometimes I listen to those Books on Tape. Y'ever read *Raise the Titanic?*"

"Saw the movie," offered Jeremy.

Back at the office, which was a mobile home past the end of the lumberyard, Bill said: "This is a growing company." He gestured at a little window above and behind Jeremy's head, which looked out on the lot. "This isn't that seasonal position I was telling your dad about a few months back. There's guys been here ten, twenty years. I try to hire people who can see themselves retiring from Veatch & Son."

You can kind of see it coming, the life you begin assembling in these awkward moments when somebody's getting ready to offer you a job. In Hollywood, these moments sometimes present themselves as a crossroads in a cautionary tale, where the hero comes to think of himself as having been rescued, in that one moment, from the grinding boredom of an unvarying daily regimen of unglamorous tasks. Fate steps in, or chance, or providence, and reveals his purpose, his calling, the shining vistas and curious byroads of his destiny. When the spectre of the monotony he's escaped sometimes rises in memory, it's like childhood: another time entirely, a planet to which you can never return after leaving, a womb that nourished you until you were ready to breathe on your own.

But this isn't Hollywood. It's Des Moines. Jeremy didn't feel fear when he thought about life at Veatch & Son. He felt—what was the word?—inspired. "I'll be honest, I haven't thought about retirement much," he said. Both men smiled. "But this is the kind of job I feel like I'd retire from. When I was retiring. Down the road. You know, when it gets to that point."

"When it gets to that point," Veatch agreed. "Listen, let me show you the warehouse. There's a whole picking system you'll want to learn."

On the way home to Nevada his thoughts began to organize themselves very quickly; there were only two open courses of action. He could take the job with Bill and quit Video Hut, or he could turn down the job and stay where he was. Beyond these lay only variations. None of the variations had any meat on their bones.

He overshot his turn at sixty-five miles an hour. At first he put it down to distraction, but as he made his way back along old Highway 30 from Colo, he realized where he was going: to Sarah Jane's, to talk. He didn't have the specific shape of their talk outlined clearly; in earlier days, this would have stayed his hand. He didn't like to start talking before he knew what he meant to say. But there was a need to act in this moment before it passed. The defining characteristic of moments, he knew, is that they pass. The whole detour took him a solid hour, all told; there was an accident backing up traffic in the no-man's-land between towns, two fire engines and an ambulance and an officer in the middle of the highway directing traffic. Jeremy always felt wrong just driving past a pileup; he felt like men of an earlier age would have gotten out to help. But the flashing lights and the burning flares seemed to send the specific message *stay out of the way.*

Sarah Jane wasn't home, of course. She was in Collins affixing lengths of masking tape to empty canning jars that would be filled with jam as the year progressed. She sat in a wooden chair next to a tall shelf in the basement, a crate full of jars at her feet and a red Sharpie in one hand. Her lettering hand repeated one of four movements with each pass, and that movement told the shelving hand what to do next. *S* for strawberry. *B* for the blueberries that would come in summer. *P* for autumn pears and *PP* for pumpkin butter. The reduplicated *P* didn't offend her eye like *PB* did; she'd made an executive decision.

Once a jar'd been labeled, she slid it back as far on a shelf as it would go: nimbly, then, her hand would dart back into the crate. The whole process took less than a minute. It was quiet work and it went quickly. All lined up, label sides facing out, the empty jars waited for someone to come along and give meaning to their name tags. Prior to the actual canning their red letters might have meant anything, who knows what. Of course, no one who didn't already know what they stood for was ever going to see them, so it didn't really matter, but it gets easy to let your mind wander, doing simple busywork in a basement. The gentle scraping sound of the jar bottom on the wooden shelf. The simple solitude.

People tell stories about video stores and the clerks who spend multiple summers at their counters, marking time, or about the owners, the ranch houses they live in, the Nissans in their driveways. People also tell stories about houses out in the country, old farmhouses, sitting unprepossessingly on large lots parceled out a century ago, soaking up darkness from depths in the earth past those where you'd till. They tell you the history of the house, who built it, what the town was like when it went up, how things seemed after everybody'd moved on to the bigger cities or set out for new land.

If you sift through the stories a narrative begins to emerge that's hard to convey in general terms, but I am reminded of it when I watch the third scene on the tape marked *Shed #4*. There are several people in this scene, at least three, though it's hard to be sure because of the hoods, which can't really properly be called "hoods": they're just some old sheets with a little binding below the jaw end. The people wearing them mill about, or try to, their hands in front of them—looking for a door? Trying not to bump into each other? But they do bump into each other; they always draw back politely when it happens. Their movement slows. It's clear that the most they can see through their masks is a faint hint of shadow. They begin again.

No one seems to be minding the camera; after a while, one of the guests runs into the tripod, and the two fall together to the dirt floor. The camera is then trained by chance on the hooded face, which has a floral pattern. It's a pillowcase, I think. I can't remember. The others run into the fallen figure, but hold themselves upright, recalculating their rough parabolas, trying to make sense of the new data.

Shed #4 was not made available for commercial release, though a few seconds from it ended up on either *Tango & Cash* or *Mortal Thoughts*. The master tape is quite long, and makes for tiresome viewing, but it's not without its moments of pathos. Eventually everybody is on the floor. That is really the only possible outcome of *Shed #4*, whose title might refer to four sheds, in which case new assumptions have to be made about the property in Collins, or to the tape itself being the fourth in a series, which seems more likely, though this shed does seem a little smaller than the one we're used to. Could be a function of population, though. When there's more people in a room it just looks smaller to the eye. Fill it up with a whole bunch of people and you'd hardly be able to make out the details of the shed at all.

11 "Your dad's told me a lot about you," Shauna Kinzer said at the dinner table the following night. It was true. Steve Heldt talked about Jeremy every chance he got—about how he hoped things would work out with Bill Veatch; about how he was glad to still have his son in the house, even though it sometimes seemed like the time for a change was coming; about the movies they watched together. There was quiet power in the way she listened to him—patiently, not waiting to break in, hearing his story coalesce around a profusion of small details. He felt at ease telling her about himself. When he spoke, she'd watch his face, and when he did go quiet, she'd ask questions, good ones. He tended to smooth over dense growth with a high gloss of facts and figures—place names, lineages, simple chronologies. She kept bringing him back into the picture. "So where are you in all this?" she'd asked at one lunch when he'd started down some line of dates and places; later, back at work, he supposed it was time she met his son.

Jeremy smiled and gave a very small nod. His father was orchestrating something tonight that didn't really compare with anything he'd tried before; Jeremy could sense it. It was just dinner, but there was more to it than that. Preparing for it—inviting Shauna, readying Jeremy, accepting it as a natural next step—had involved instinct and intuition: there weren't any domestic suppliers for these. You had to import them from someplace.

So he felt proud of his dad. He picked up the dish of scalloped potatoes Steve had asked him to get ready that afternoon.

"Potatoes?" he said.

"Thank you," said Shauna, helping herself.

"Dad says you're from Nebraska," offered Jeremy.

"Yes, Lincoln."

"Cornhuskers," said Jeremy.

"'Go Big Red,'" She nodded. "I used to play a little softball, actually."

Steve reached for the pot roast. "She's being modest. Her team went to the tournament in '84."

"No kidding," said Jeremy.

"Down in Omaha," said Shauna. "We came in second."

"No kidding," said Jeremy again, comfortably, easily.

"They call it the World Series but it's really a bracket. We beat Fresno State but we drew Texas A&M in the next round."

"They play a lot of baseball in Texas," Steve offered.

"Softball, too," said Shauna.

"Softball, too," said Steve. Jeremy looked up from his plate to see his father exchanging a smile with Shauna. Some in-joke, maybe. From the way they looked at each other, you'd have thought they were old friends.

"Where did you meet her?" she asked while they were all bringing their plates into the kitchen; she was looking at a family portrait on the wall above the microwave. In it, a younger Jeremy held an oversized wooden alphabet block on his lap, its big blue H facing the camera. His parents were standing on either side of him; Mom, in a sleeveless beige summer dress with yellow trim, had her hand on his shoulder.

"Just growing up, just from around," Steve said.

"That's nice," said Shauna. She meant it; you grow up and it gets harder to meet people, but there are shrinking places in the world where the people you meet growing up are the people you know later on. These places seem less nice when you feel trapped in them, but once you get free they seem sweet. "You all look so happy."

Jeremy didn't mean to hold his breath for a half second: it just happened, there at the top of the inhale. "Mom was excited for the pictures," he said, letting it go. "They were doing Christmas scenes too if you wanted to get your Christmas cards made there, so we did those. We were giving her a little bit of a hard time about it."

"About Christmas?"

"About how when they brought out the tree you could see her getting really excited."

"Like a kid," said Steve.

Jeremy felt pressure in his temples, psychic strain, the sort of stuff he'd once been adept at evading. The moment was tugging at him like it had a hook in the roof of his mouth: they could all stay there, they could see what else might come out. But he picked up a green sponge and turned the water on in the sink.

"Dad, could you put the rest of the potatoes in the Tupperware?" he said.

"I've got it," said Shauna.

At sixty-five miles an hour, the cornfields flicker against the window like stock footage; shadows in between the rows pulse steadily in shades of yellow and green and early brown. There are as many bean fields now as corn, but nobody remembers those, their rows green and spiky and nearer to the ground. Corn, though: it hoists itself skyward all by itself, determinate, until the long green leaves on the stalks grow heavy and begin to droop in autumn. From the road it's like a painting, a huge mural, endless, ongoing.

You see cars pulled over and people who've gotten out to take pictures sometimes, around midday—families or couples who're driving cross-country. There's plenty of corn west in Nebraska, of course, and more of it east in Illinois, but there's something about these gently rolling fields that makes people want to get a closer look. Near sunset, long, wheeling shadows suggest a different sort of picture, one with maybe a quiet hint of menace to it. But by then most of the people taking pictures have moved on.

The highway abutting the fields is miraculously uniform for miles on end; this is true on both the east-west and the north-south routes. Are they separate fields on either side of the highway, or does the road mark an artificial division through a single, uniform field? It's a stupid question, because it only matters to whoever owns the land, but you get all kinds of thoughts when the sun's strobe-lighting through the driver's side window all day; and if you let yourself start thinking about the field without the highway, some-thing happens to the way you take in the land. Your inner vision shifts. You think about fields with no one to see them, all that quiet life continuing on with no purpose beyond self-propagation. Tas-sels rotting in October. It gets to you, if you let it.

But instead of just driving the whole way from border to bor-der, let's say you get out into the rows, where the growth is thick and tall enough to dampen sound. You notice this effect even be-fore you begin to speak; your ears register how the air's a little dif-ferent. "Hello!" people yell, making sure it's not just some vague feeling they have, or "Is this Heaven?" They don't mean that;

they're quoting from a movie about a man who builds a baseball field to coax the ghosts of old baseball players into emerging from the corn. There are other times when people go into the fields and yell different things: "Help!" for example, often repeatedly with increasing volume, or "Where are you taking me?" But nobody usually hears them. A few rows of corn will muffle the human voice so effectively that, even a few insignificant rows away, all is silence, what to speak of out at the highway's shoulder: all the way back there, already fading into memory now. To make yourself heard, you'd need something substantial: the roar of the combine harvester in autumn, mowing all of this to the ground, and then rolling back over the stubble like a ruthless conqueror from an alien planet. Or something greater, bigger, louder. An airplane. But nobody's going to land any airplanes out here.

"Farmer?" Jeremy was saying, with an air that made him sound older than he was; it made his father feel proud. "He's got one tractor, no help except one son, and he's a farmer?" They had adjourned to the living room and were watching *Blue Chips*, which was a movie about basketball; Nick Nolte was trying to recruit a high school player from rural Louisiana. It was one of the most popular tapes in the store; they had to stock four copies just to keep up with demand. Even then, one went missing.

Shauna smiled. "'Family farms,' right?"

"Yeah," said Steve. "Weird they wouldn't make him a shrimp fisherman or something."

"Rice, though," said Jeremy. "Rice for export."

Steve pointed at the screen. "Awful dry for growing rice."

"There's no way that's actually Louisiana," said Shauna.

"Tractor but no truck," Steve said. He tried not to let his face show how much he was enjoying himself, from the dinner table through coffee afterward down to the present moment, gathered together on the sofa and chairs in front of the TV in the living room. "Just the one tractor."

"These movies aren't really for people who've been around farms," said Jeremy, a little apologetically, and then the screen rippled.

It was a static shot: the frame held, impartial and austere, in marked contrast to the hand-held scenes in the shed. She was running. There was no need for anyone to give chase; it was the middle of the night on a long gravel driveway abutting a corn field, and the woman, fleeing, had only rough moonlight to guide her . . . where? Across the highway? Into the road? She ran, canvas hood in hand, growing smaller as she made progress, the sound of her footfalls fading into silence.

Steve Heldt leaned toward the screen, a helpless look on his face.

"That—that's your mother," he said.

"No, Dad," said Jeremy.

"You think I don't recognize my own wife," said Steve.

"It's not her, Dad."

"What?" said Shauna.

"It's her," he said. He was rising involuntarily to his feet, his body drawn to the vanishing figure in the dark.

"No," said Jeremy. He was reaching for the remote. "There's a bunch of tapes like this. A couple, anyway. I've seen her before. It's not Mom." The screen popped white for a half second before the darkness became general. Steve kept his eyes trained on the screen, an unwilling cartographer of lost locales, invisible ink on a wrinkled map turning brown in the heat—look, there. Those landmasses out there in the middle of the water. These are new.

Shauna was at the wall switch. "Probably some kids with a camcorder," she said, shaking her head. "It's a different world now. Should I make some decaf?"

Jeremy's thoughts were swimming in several directions. *I like you and I hope you take care of my dad.* He didn't say it out loud, of course. But he felt it, raw and uncomfortable, as Shauna Kinzer restored order to a room that had, only minutes earlier, been under attack.

12 They had shredded wheat the next morning, at the same kitchen table where, nine hours earlier, they'd watched Shauna work, as if the damage that needed undoing had been hers to atone for. She'd stood, sometimes pacing, while the two men sat and listened; she'd spoken, not excitedly but patiently, gathering up the few available threads and spinning them together into a working theory about the strange scenes on the tapes.

She was magnificent. In the dark, she'd seen Steve in his half-crouch before the screen, desperate; in the kitchen, where they'd gathered, she buried that moment, using small talk and idle guesses for shovels. Jeremy broke in from time to time with rough descriptions of the other scenes he'd watched; she drew them all together.

"It could even be something to get people excited about a movie that hasn't come out yet," she said at one point. "I don't know if either of you saw that *Blair Witch Project* but they had something like this on the Internet." Both nodded back. She worked easily, gently, until the still-developing evening's earlier act began to feel remote and distant. By 10:30 she had constructed a pretty sturdy comfort zone out of available materials.

"Sorry about last night," Steve said to Jeremy now, not looking up from his cereal.

"First one of those scenes I ever saw, I'll tell you what," Jeremy said. "I couldn't even sleep. Stayed awake all night. Nothing to be sorry about."

Steve gave an almost wordless nod; there's a noise some men make with their mouths closed when they're ready to place a ridge-marker in a conversation but don't know how. Most mornings the TV was on—news, weather. It was quiet today. The sky came through the kitchen window blue and grand and full of possibilities, which happens everywhere, but not every day: just some days.

"So I got offered that job with Bill Veatch," Jeremy said. "I was going to mention it last night, but—"

"Well, congratulations," Steve broke in. "Proud of you. They give you a start date? You need work clothes?"

"Slow down a little," said Jeremy. "I told him I have to talk to Sarah Jane."

"To put in notice, you mean."

"Well, to talk first, but sure." Jeremy couldn't put into words what he meant when he said he had to talk to Sarah Jane: it was something about holding patterns and the itching persistence of loose ends, the relative ease of knowing where they're located. The nearness of everything in his life to the house where they'd all once been a family. Fixed points in space and time.

"Well, all right," said Steve, and then: "I think your mom would be proud, too."

It always sat a little funny with Jeremy: Dad speaking on Mom's behalf in her absence. These past few years of sitting around waiting for something to solidify: wouldn't Mom have also understood that? You wait for signs, but there aren't any signs; you wait a while longer, just in case.

"You think so?" said Jeremy.

"I do think so," his father said. "You'll be making a life for yourself. That's what any mother wants for her children."

Jeremy did not have a name for the feeling in his chest when he heard his father say this; it registered as a physical sensation, hard and solid, like a stone lodged in his sternum underneath the skin, something that had been there long enough for him to stop thinking about it most of the time but whose weight registered now, coolly radiating through his chest. He nodded, grunted, made sure to look his father in the eyes. Soon all of this will be gone.

He stopped past Sarah Jane's place first, on his way in to work. He wanted to tell her in person he was sorry to leave, and that he was grateful for the chance she'd taken on him back when he was just a junior at Nevada High. Of course anybody could work the counter at Video Hut, but that wasn't the point. In his dream of the person he hoped to become, you always thanked the people who'd helped you along. It was important.

But of course there was no car in the driveway, nobody home. Stopping by was only paying courtesy to a shared fiction, a head-nod to the silence around Sarah Jane's increasingly long absences from the store. The place felt abandoned. Somebody'd been keeping up appearances—mowing the lawn, sweeping the porch, emptying the mailbox—but it wasn't enough. The windows looked lifeless.

For a while he let the engine idle at the curb, watching the door of the house and measuring his options. She still made occasional appearances at the store; at least once a week she'd turn up, usually around closing time on weeknights. He could just wait until their paths crossed, but he didn't want to. The momentum he felt was real. It was time.

So he kept in mind what mothers want for their sons as he dialed Sarah Jane from the work phone. He felt guilty; leaving Video Hut now felt a little like jumping ship. He and Ezra held down the fort these days, but the whole operation was in disrepair. There was no action, no forward motion. In February, they'd come in one morning to find a new sheet taped to the counter next to the A.M. OPEN page: it said EMERGENCY CONTACTS, but there was only one number on it, *SARAH JANE (cell)*, with a redundant *only contact in case of extreme emergency!* underneath. When did she get a cell phone? He didn't want to call it.

You've reached the voice mail of Sarah Jane Shepherd. I'm unable to take your call at this time, ran the message. This was followed by a man's voice, distorted, too cheerful, announcing: *The mailbox belonging to*—and here Sarah Jane jumped back in: *Sarah Jane Shepherd,* blunt, declamatory—*is full. Please try again later.*

He set the phone back in its cradle. After a while the door jingled; it was Joan from Mary Greeley. "Late night?" she said.

Jeremy realized he'd been staring off into space. "Not lately," he said, finding the surface quickly, glad of it.

They talked awhile about how many nice days might be left in the year before it got too humid. He kept pace, but it took some effort. The whole conversation felt like it belonged to another era, a time of reliable coefficients, and his mind was on Collins now: on trying, before he moved on, to get some glimpse of what had disturbed Video Hut's once-inviolate stillness, its perennial motionless static present, a thing already passing into legend.

"You sleeping all right up there? Gets pretty hot, if I remember."

"I'm fine. It's not humid enough yet to stay hot all night."

"Well, if you want one of the other rooms—"

"I've always wanted an attic room, is the thing, so it's nice to spend a few nights in one," Sarah Jane said. "When I was a little girl—"

"We had a basement," Lisa interrupted. "Nobody else on our street had one. It stayed cool in summer."

"Right. My grandfather had one, too. He kept the freezer down there, had whole sides of beef in it. We weren't allowed to play around in the basement."

"Well," Lisa said, "if it gets too hot, these old farmhouses are huge. Two of the other rooms I'm just using for storage, I could clear them out."

The breakfast table was in the kitchen; it was a two-seater with a Formica top in turquoise riddled with looping white squiggles all over. It looked like it had enjoyed a quiet life at a diner; it was an antique, but not a showpiece. People pay a lot of money now for reproductions of tables like these, but plenty of them are gathering dust at auction houses if you know where to look. Raise up the two leaves that hang down on either side of it and it'll seat four.

Centered on the wall above it was an old black-and-white photograph in an oval frame: a carhop at a drive-in, somewhere in the Midwest in a bygone era, her uniform crisp, square hat set neatly atop her hair worn in a bun. The picture had been personalized in gloriously legible cursive script: *You're always welcome back at Henry's! Love, Irene.*

"I don't really know why I put the guest room in the attic," she said after a moment. "The view, maybe."

"That view in the morning is really something," Sarah Jane offered.

"It's nice at night, too. The window faces the moon as it rises."

"I'll watch for it."

81

She cleared their plates and stood at the sink, rinsing. The air smelled like sausage.

"Are you going back in today?"

Sarah Jane blinked. "Of course."

"Are you going to get your things?"

Another blink, and a breath. "Am I moving in?"

"I have a lot of work to do around here," Lisa said. "You already know a little about the business." The kitchen window faced the east; the whole room was flooded with sunlight, clean and summery.

"I'll bring some things," said Sarah Jane.

The wind comes across the plains not howling but singing. It's the difference between this wind and its big-city cousins: the full-throated wind of the plains has leeway to seek out the hidden registers of its voice. Where immigrant farmers planted windbreaks a hundred and fifty years ago, it keens in protest; where the young corn shoots up, it whispers as it passes, crossing field after field in its own time, following eastward trends but in no hurry to find open water. You can't usually see it in paintings, but it's an important part of the scenery.

Every spring it's like a puppy: always more energy than you remembered, leaping to life from an afternoon nap. You can feel it battering the windshield if you're driving into it, and at night it might make you worry, but in the daytime it's bracing. It felt, today, in Jeremy's body as he drove down Highway 65, like a validation of his course, like the world responding to his choices with a palpable *yes*. Yes, it was time to launch out into the world, to set a course for the future. Yes, it was all right that he'd called Stephanie Parsons to tell her he'd been wrong, that he did actually want to know the address of the house; it was all right, when she teased him a little about it, to enjoy it. Was it all right to go try to find Sarah Jane instead of just waiting for her to show up at work? Yes, even if it wasn't really in his character to just get in the car and head south. But yes decisively to all of this, driving out to Collins.

He turned the radio up when the signal from Des Moines shrugged off the last of the static, and he let the window down a little. The air rushed in. He was leaning his head into the wind when he saw the blue Chevrolet in the ditch to the side of the road, clumps of long grass out on the blacktop ahead of it.

There was broken glass arcing out in a half-moon from its front end, and a big greenish pool from where the radiator'd burst or been punctured. All four wheels were still. It looked like a great dead insect on its back. It was Ezra's car, and it was upside down.

In later years he could find nothing in the gap between seeing the wreck and finding himself outside the car, on his knees, lifting Ezra's body by the shoulders even though he'd been told in Health and Safety class just a few years ago not to touch anything at the scene of an accident unless you meant to begin CPR. On the asphalt were dozens of VHS tapes without their cases, some crushed, either by impact with the road when they'd been thrown from the car or by the car rolling over them. Loose tape rippled in the wind.

Jeremy wasn't yelling; he wasn't the kind of person to just start yelling. But he could hear his voice rising in pitch. "What are you doing all the way out here?" The sound of it in his own ears unnerved him: that loss of control, the first tentative steps toward panic. "Are you lost, are you lost?" he kept asking, repeating himself each time he got no answer. Ezra's house was clear over on the other side of Ames toward Boone. It was as if he'd meant to head out toward where he lived but gone in the wrong direction.

Ezra was in no position to explain himself. He had lost a lot of blood. His eyes were half-open, and he seemed to recognize that somebody he knew was with him, but he said nothing. He drew great, deep breaths at intervals. The sky above was showing early afternoon flashes of orange, its constant variations flooding the horizon in changing color bars like on the title screen from that weird Charles Bronson movie, the one where he steals a sword from Toshiro Mifune on a train. *Red Sun*.

PART TWO

✳

1   Lisa Sample was born in Tama in 1969. Before she came to Collins she'd lived most of her life, as she told Sarah Jane the first day they met, in Pottawattamie County, which is quite some ways from Tama. Her father'd worked for a while with cattlemen in Omaha. His whole family had lived in Crescent, just across the Mormon Bridge.

It was her mother, Irene, who'd originally come from Tama; after the baby was born, she'd moved west for the second and last time. She packed what she wanted to keep into two old suitcases and left the rest of her room in state: a bed with a floral coverlet, an oak lampstand, a chair too big to fit into the Chevrolet. "All the furniture you'll ever want back in Walnut," Peter Sample had said cheerfully, trying to put a good face on it: Walnut was an hour's drive from Crescent and full of antique stores. But to Irene leaving Tama was like sawing down a whole brace of trees that shielded a house from the wind. "Almost Nebraska," Lisa'd said to Sarah Jane to help her locate Pottawattamie County in her mind. She meant to emphasize its remoteness, but also to keep her claim where it belonged: in Iowa, where she was born.

Irene Colton had lived away from Tama before; she wasn't entirely rootbound. In 1957, she'd won a scholarship to Ottumwa

Heights College. It was during her senior year there that she met Peter Sample. He was changing trains on the way home from Chicago, where he'd spent the week at a cattlemen's convention; every weekend she picked up one shift at Henry's Drive-In. It was Sunday. He sat at the counter and ordered a hamburger with cole-slaw and mashed potatoes, but when he got out his Bankameri-card to pay the bill, Irene pointed at the CASH ONLY sign on the counter. He was embarrassed, but she reached into her apron. "It's on me," she said; her smile looked genuine because it was.

A week later her manager brought her an envelope addressed to her; tucked inside a greeting card with a picture of Omaha on the front were three one-dollar bills. *Greetings from Omaha*, it said on the front, and, inside, in admirably neat handwriting: "Thanks for lunch. Hope to see you if I pass through again."

Idly, just for fun, she wrote back to him at the return address on the envelope, thanking him; "Everybody loves the story of the Omaha man who sent me three dollars," she said. About a month later, she got another letter, and when she answered that one he wrote back again. His letters were all substance, but light fare: pleasant, harmless, transparent thoughts from a young man who lived alone and worked around cattle. He spoke with the assumed familiarity of the irredeemably local: the guy who owns the Texaco opened up a used-car lot behind the station, I'm thinking about buying a station wagon from him; the city bought a new snow-plow and the chief of police personally drives it; the Dillow family is selling their house, it's hard to believe, their name goes back around here for generations. It felt like he needed somebody to talk to; reading his gentle unburdenings made her feel like she was doing somebody some good, which she liked.

In college she'd known plenty of boys who had Peter Sample beat for worldliness, even though he'd seen more of the world than they had; but she reckoned this in his favor, not theirs. His courtship was obvious and awkward, and felt of a piece with the small-town manners she'd learned as a child: the easy touch of the everyday, the pervasive mild formality. In the autumn of 1963, he visited Tama, taking an extra day on his way to a conference he didn't really need to attend. Her family liked him.

She'd worked all summer doing clerical work for a dentist; it didn't seem like a great use of her education, but she wasn't sure what else she was supposed to do with her life. So when Peter's visits began to observe a predictable quarterly pattern, following the seasons, Irene was receptive. One spring he brought a carton of frozen steaks packed in dry ice: "I get them at cost," he said, not wanting to seem extravagant. Still, her father relished making the same joke at the table several times over the next month: "I feel like the president!" he said.

Over Christmas 1965 he stayed two whole weeks at the Hotel Toledo; he'd made senior accountant at the stockyard and had plenty of time on the books. On the Sunday before Christmas, he joined the family in worship at Grace Evangelical. The services were mild and gentle, wholly devoid of proselytizing, and he didn't mind them at all; the choir sang "Pass Me Not, O Gentle Savior" while the ushers passed the collection plate. Irene stood singing with a soft, contented look in her green eyes, holding the hymnal open but never looking down to check the lyrics. Peter took note. She'd mentioned Bible camp in talking about her childhood, but only in passing.

He was conscious of not wanting to wear out his welcome at the Colton household, so he spent many hours alone in his room that December; it had a television, but he didn't like to watch much television. Instead, he sat and thought, in a nice old chair that came with the room: he thought to himself about what he was doing in Tama, and what he ought to maybe do next. He tried to diagram the natural course of events between himself and Irene. He wrote down a few notes on hotel stationery, rough projected timelines extending into the future, but these do not survive.

Over time he became a familiar face in Tama. He'd stay for a weekend at the Toledo every few months, visiting the Coltons, going to church on Sunday morning with Irene; her mother and father stayed home except for holidays now, but Irene loved how the light came through the stained-glass scenes in the high church windows, and Peter didn't mind. He stole glances at her when she bowed her head to pray, her eyebrows knitted in concentration; and he wondered to himself about the substance of her silent prayers, though he never asked. He did not pray himself but sat respectfully. Before heading home, he'd treat the whole family to dinner out.

Around town, he developed a reputation for being a little stuffy; his manners had been formed in a vanishing time. There was speculation, if not outright gossip, about whether he'd take Irene away somewhere, but he held to his pattern for over a year, nearly two. In December 1967, after knowing her for four years and having become a seasonal fixture at the table in her parents' house, he proposed marriage at the dinner table in front of the whole family, and she said yes.

"We don't have to leave Tama right away," he told her the next morning when they went for a walk; he knew it would be hard for her to leave. She was thankful for a husband-to-be who was considerate and understanding, who also came from a small town. But when they explained the plan to her parents at dinner that night, her father grew stern.

"That's a waste of money," he said to Peter, as if there were no one else in the room.

"It's an expense," conceded Peter. "But it's a temporary expense."

"It's a waste," said Harold Colton. "Either you should move here, or you both should move out to Crescent." Irene's mother nodded without looking up from her plate.

"He's right," Irene said. She was of two minds about leaving home: since coming home from college, she'd felt restless, a little curious about what else there might be beyond Tama, having seen just enough at college to pique her interest. But living a whole day's drive from her parents made her anxious, the idea of it; they weren't old yet, but it wouldn't be long. Her job wasn't awful, but she didn't care about it; starting a new life appealed to her, but she couldn't wholly envision the particulars, and when she tried, she felt uneasy. Still, college had been fun, every year a little more so; she pictured herself out in western Iowa, going into Omaha on weekends, seeing the sights. And she wanted to be bold and decisive, to make an impression on Peter like the one she'd made when they first met.

"You have a good job," she said; her father nodded with satisfaction. "That's where we ought to settle down."

But Crescent was not Ottumwa. She made a few friends and played bridge with them, braiding simple daily threads together into a new life that didn't feel entirely unfamiliar. For a while she felt as if she were settling in; but toward the end of her pregnancy's first trimester, in 1968, she began to feel an almost primal nervousness, a need to be near her family. She wanted her mother's meat loaf, not some meat loaf made using her mother's recipe but the very one stirred together by her mother in a purple glass bowl on the tiny kitchen counter and baked for an hour and fifteen minutes in the Magic Chef oven. She hadn't acclimated to the view from the living room window in Crescent: it still felt like somebody

91

else's window, somebody else's yard. She couldn't lay claim to it in her mind. The feeling gnawed at her as her body grew bigger; she didn't want to have her baby in a strange hospital far away. It is hard to leave home, and sometimes it takes a long time.

"The faucet's broken again," Irene said to Peter at dinner.

"Seems like there's always something with this place," he said. It was true; he'd secured a job at the Tama Bank & Trust before leaving Crescent, but it didn't pay like the Union Stockyards. They'd left a lot of money behind.

"I washed the plates in the bathtub," she said. In her high chair, Lisa Sample gave out a joyful cry and slapped the mashed peas on her tray with an open palm. She was eight months old.

"Do you want me to give Henry a call?" Henry Jordan owned the house they rented, along with two other houses in town; he kept up the maintenance on them himself. Irene tried to avoid bothering him too much. He was a nice old man and she felt like he needed his rest.

"I don't know," she said.

Peter put down his fork and smiled at the baby, who smiled back through a mouthful of food. "You know," he said, eyes still on his daughter, splitting his tone between business and baby talk, "back in Crescent I hear the Ketterman house is for sale. They've got a sink as big as a fishing hole, yes they do." He tickled Lisa's chin; she cooed.

"Peter," she said.

"I know," he said, still playing at baby talk. "But we're throwing money away, staying out here. Throw-throw-throwing money. Yes we are!" The appeal to thrift was fair play, and a reliable arrow in the quiver.

"But we manage," she said.

"I know we do," he said, turning finally. "And I don't mind. I don't. I know you like to be near your parents."

Lisa cleared what remained of her peas from her tray in one sudden sweep of her short, plump arm; they sprayed across the room like heavy confetti.

Irene was reaching for a dish towel.

"Terry called from the stockyards and says the new guy already left," he said. "He asked me to reconsider."

"She won't eat the carrots, either," she said, smiling up from her position on the floor. "Carrots are easier to pick up."

"There'd be room enough for another baby, if we wanted one," he said.

Irene had crushed several peas under her knees cleaning up the mess; scowling, she calculated the time she'd have to waste on the carpet after putting the baby to bed.

"I feel like I'm just getting up on my feet again, Peter," she said. She remembered Crescent as a place where everything looked familiar but never felt that way.

"Well, OK," he said, cheerfully, like he'd only been floating a mild suggestion. But the germ was in the grain. The next day Henry Jordan forgot all about the sink; it was Wednesday before he got to it, and all the while the interior of the Ketterman house grew fine and fresh in her mind. Clean counters, shiny showerheads. It couldn't be all that much better than this, she knew, but a little might go a long way. And so it was Irene, the following week, who next raised the question of moving house, which she did by first telling Peter how grateful she was that she'd been able to have her baby at home; but it was important, wasn't it, to start saving up for college, because time would get away from them before they knew it and costs were going up every year, et cetera.

They'd been in Tama less than a year. Away, then back, now away again. So much news. It's important to consider your choices carefully before settling on a course of action; when you keep changing course, you forget where you are. It's disorienting.

Lisa Sample celebrated her second birthday with her family on October 9, 1970, gleefully smashing both hands facedown into a two-layer vanilla cake with pink frosting, baked by her mother, Irene, at their home, the former Ketterman place in Crescent, Iowa, population 856.

2   On the living room carpet in Crescent, Irene was trying to teach Lisa to play Parcheesi. Lisa couldn't follow the action, but she loved the dice, the way they rattled in the little blue cup. Was three too young for board games? Her mother thought probably so, but Lisa'd arrived at every milestone early: weaned early, crawled early, and surprised everybody with her first word before she could walk ("bear!" while having *The Little Engine That Could* read aloud to her; the bear in question was scratching at a tree on the same hillside where the train stalled). As soon as she could say two simple sentences she began putting them together to tell stories about her dolls: "They stopped playing. They need a rest," she explained to her mother once, sequestering a Raggedy Ann in one corner of the living room and a nameless blinking-eyed vinyl doll in the one opposite.

In town there were only a few other little girls her age. Everybody knew everybody else. The kids would play together while the mothers visited, sometimes at one house, sometimes at another; there was a single grocery store that served as a social hub most mornings. It was a good life, small and navigable.

Peter got home early; it was four. He wasn't due home until six thirty. "Daddy!" Lisa yelled, running to hug his knees.

"I haven't even started dinner," Irene said apologetically, getting up, but this was strictly a formal protest: Peter's commute, and the way it meant they only occasionally took the evening meal all together, was a hardship for her. She had grown up in a house where everyone met at the table at the end of the day.

"They let us out early to buy gas," he said, in motion, picking up Lisa and rubbing noses with her before putting her back down. She ran back to the Parcheesi board. Irene knitted her brow.

"To buy *gas?*"

He took a folded copy of the *Omaha World-Herald* from the pocket of his fall coat. "Prices doubled overnight," he said. "Cars lined up two blocks down the street from the station."

Irene read the headline and skimmed the story: it had a sidebar about the best times to avoid long lines. "That's crazy," she said.

"It's *crazy*," he said. "People are bringing their own cans to carry away extra. The guys at the station were trying to discourage it, but people are determined." Lisa was at the Parcheesi board throwing dice from the shaker again and again, saying the numbers out loud.

"What in the world," said Irene.

"Politics," he said. "All the oil used to come from Texas. I just paid twelve dollars for a tank of gas."

"What on *earth*," she said.

"Well, I know, but I can't exactly walk to work from here," he said: that light tone, the easy cheer. It was his strength. "Could get worse by next week. I filled it up. It's an expense for now."

"Nine!" said Lisa.

"An expense, sure," said Irene, wheels turning: in two months they were supposed to drive home to Tama for Christmas.

"Just a short-term situation, most likely," he said. "Back in July

96

when the car was in the shop I rode in with Bill. We could try that some more."

Irene started hurrying around the kitchen, pulling a few steaks from the freezer. "That will be nice," she said.

"Sure," he said. "Some company on the way in is nice."

"Twelve!" Lisa cried in triumph.

"How many twelves is that?" her father asked.

"First one!" she said.

A lot of people have never really been to a small town, not even to stop for gas. They have ideas about how small towns should look: they're supposed to have maybe only one building taller than two stories, usually the bank, standing tall in the middle of a two-block downtown. There'll be a school and a high school and a grocery store and a library, and maybe a department store and maybe a Texaco and a Shell. More people on the sidewalks than cars on the streets. Several parks with swings and slides and baseball diamonds.

There are towns like that in Iowa, plenty of them; Nevada fits the bill. More than six thousand people live there, and the sign on the Lincoln Highway that welcomes you there declares Nevada the "26th best small town in America." It has soil testing labs, water testing labs, a high school football team. There's a little espresso and cappuccino place just outside of downtown. Java Time. People shoot scenes for movies on soundstages and try to make it look like Nevada, but the claustrophobia they're trying to invoke is more native to a place like Crescent, whose length you can walk in a day.

It's not a ghost town; there are a couple of motels, and a restaurant or two. There's a church, and a bar. There are just fewer of these places than you usually think of when you picture a town where people go to live. If you were to visit for a weekend, you'd be able to see all of it on foot; and you might say, later, that it looked like there was hardly anything there—that you didn't know what people did there, why they didn't just move into Omaha. I don't think I could live there, you might say. But it's more likely that you won't have occasion to say any of this, because you won't visit Crescent at all, unless you maybe have family there, which, statistically speaking, you probably don't.

The Samples were spending their Saturday morning in Omaha, down at the Old Market; for a while they'd been able to come in every weekend, but after the gas crunch hit they made it every other weekend. They'd had their usual big breakfast; Lisa finished about half of her pancakes and was presently running around in a toy store while her parents browsed the shelves. Everything seemed a little pricey. Irene remembered her mother telling her they raised the prices right before Christmas.

"Keep an eye on Lisa," she said to Peter, retrieving her coin purse from her handbag. "I'm going to make sure there's still time on the meter."

"I don't think they'll ticket you if we run just a little over," he said.

"I'm just going to go check the meter," she said.

There were still eight minutes left on it when she got to the car; she put another dime in. Better safe than sorry. On the sidewalk a few meters down she saw a young man with a beard reaching into a garbage can. He had a long army-green overcoat on; it was wrinkled and dirty. She could see the crust of a sandwich poking up from the coat's breast pocket.

The scene made her feel terrible; it was November now, and

getting colder, and the shop windows were all lit up with Christmas scenes and snowflakes. In her purse was a doggie bag with the rest of Lisa's pancakes from breakfast; they'd probably sit in the refrigerator for two days before getting thrown out, and Lisa wouldn't miss them.

"There's a little breakfast left," she said, approaching—gingerly, without making eye contact.

He took the pancakes out of the bag and began eating, quickly, with his hands. She turned away, not wanting to stare, but he said: "Ma'am?"

"It's all right," she said.

" 'To knowledge, temperance; to temperance, patience; to patience, godliness; and to godliness, brotherly kindness; and to brotherly kindness, charity,' " said the bearded man, delivering the verse very quickly, as if passing along a recipe he knew by heart. It was hard to understand him; he was still chewing. With his free hand he retrieved a crumpled tract from the pocket of his coat. "Here."

"I'm sure, yes," she said. She tucked the tract into her purse.

"We have meetings on Sundays," he said, wiping his mouth on his sleeve.

"That's fine," she said, turning now finally, heeding an uncomfortable feeling in her chest that told her it was time to go; the bearded man returned to his garbage can, rooting around shoulder-deep. But the exchange stayed with her as they rode back. She'd found a church in Crescent, but she seldom got the chance to go; she didn't like to bother Peter on his days off. He worked so hard. On their visits to Tama she thought of her attendance at Grace Evangelical as a sort of inoculation, a booster shot to carry her through next Christmas.

Outside the car the wind was blowing; Peter had to focus on

the road. Lisa sang a little song to herself whose melody Irene didn't recognize, then nodded off to sleep, and then the car was quiet, except for the engine and the sound of the wind.

This is what it said on the tract that the man eating from the garbage gave Irene:

And if thy hand serve as a snare to thee, cut it off: it is better for thee to enter into life maimed, than having thy two hands to go away into hell, into the fire unquenchable; where their worm dies not, and the fire is not quenched. And if thy foot serve as a snare to thee, cut it off: it is better for thee to enter into life lame, than having thy two feet to be cast into hell, into the fire unquenchable; where their worm dies not, and the fire is not quenched. And if thine eye serve as a snare to thee, cast it out: it is better for thee to enter into the kingdom of God with one eye, rather than having two eyes to be cast into the hell of fire, where their worm dies not, and the fire is not quenched. For every one shall be salted with fire, and every sacrifice shall be salted with salt. Salt is good, but if the salt is become saltless, wherewith will ye season it? MARK 9:43–50

We are called as witnesses to the wickedness of the last generation; as it was in the days of Noah, so also shall be the coming of the Son of Man (MT 24:37). We are called to be light unto the world, but the world apprehends it not (JN 1:5). He that receives you receives me, and he that receives me receives him that sent me (MT 10:40). Many are called ones, but few chosen ones, says the Lord (MT 22:14). We seek not Jehovah in the earthquake, nor the wind, nor in the fire, but in the still small voice that speaks to us after these things have passed (1 Kings 19:12). He who hears

100

the Word of God is of God. If God did not want to speak to you, you could not hear (JN 8:47). It is no accident that you have received this tract today.

Answer the call of the Lord who speaks to you and reject this doomed generation. You are invited to join us in worship at

—and here the print broke off, and there was a space for the zealot to rubber-stamp the name and address of his local congregation: but the space on this one was blank.

There was a drawer at the house in Crescent named after a similarly purposed drawer she'd known from the dining room service at her grandmother's house: the anything drawer. Things went there that weren't ready to be thrown away—savings account passbooks, bifocals, buttons. The day after their excursion to Omaha, cleaning out her purse, Irene read over the verse from Mark on the front of the tract. She scowled mildly—it seemed a little dour—but tucked the tract down into the anything drawer. It wouldn't take up much space. It didn't seem proper just to throw it away.

3   There weren't any preschools in Crescent just yet. Mothers who worked in Omaha or Council Bluffs found places near work to drop their kids off during the day; there were churches and private schools, all sorts of choices. But mothers who stayed in Crescent during the day had to fend for themselves. Many of them had grown up there and been friends since childhood; they made room in their web for Irene, the engine of simple social obligation humming along at its audible Midwestern frequency. Everyone was nice to Irene, and she felt welcomed, though it's one thing to feel welcome and another to feel like you belong. Irene struggled with this in the privacy of her heart, and worried sometimes that the others would somehow detect it.

To make errands easier, they all traded afternoons on Fridays; Sharon Lumley's mother would come get Lisa one week and walk both girls down the street to the Lumley house, where they were usually joined by either Gail Ehlers or Liz Gunderson. The following week all three might go instead to the Ehlers place, and the next to the Samples. The rotation gave rhythm to the increasingly busy routine of motherhood. More than three children at once was too much, they all agreed, so each week one girl stayed home with her mother; every kitchen had a calendar with off days marked in red. Particular arrangements as to who played where varied from week to week, a preventive measure against bickering.

It was April 20, 1972: Lisa's day home. She grew a little taller every day; she ate constantly—"like a boy," her father said. There was a big day ahead. She was working early with her mother in the garden behind the house: they grew beans for canning, and carrots and zucchini, and kept a small raised bed of marigolds for color. Lisa's favorite color was yellow. Fridays out in the backyard before it got too hot were magical; Lisa would rake the dirt and poke at it with her finger, her mother working while long stretches passed with no conversation, just the mellow ease of shared time.

But the garden was also a practical concern. Peter'd lost seniority when he moved to Tama; now the owners at the stockyard were reducing several positions to part-time, saying they couldn't afford to stay in Nebraska unless they contained costs. So he worked Monday through Thursday and didn't complain, but on Fridays Irene stayed out of his way. Being home and idle on a weekday made him irritable. Left to himself, he might work on small projects that kept his hands busy and left him feeling satisfied by the end of the day, but if Lisa and her friends were running around he found it hard to focus.

Trips into Omaha were rarer now. But summer would be coming soon, and Lisa needed new clothes; Irene could sew dresses, but shoes were another matter. All the other kids had sandals: she knew because Lisa had told her so. It was important that her daughter not be made to stand out from the others.

It's said that you don't retain many memories from before you turn five, but years later Lisa remembered. She was sure of it. She'd played in the garden early that morning, and later they rode into town, just the two of them. It was a Friday, her turn to be home with her mother.

Lisa's small hand tightened suddenly around Irene's index and middle fingers: she had spotted the Astro Theater across the street. Its marquee was framed by incandescent bulbs. She'd been to the movies only once in her young life, to a children's matinee at the same theater one Saturday last year; the whole family had come. For a whole week afterwards it was all she'd talked about. Even the dolls in her dollhouse had taken up the theme: "Where did you go today?" one doll would ask another. "Oh, we just went to see a movie," the other would reply, pouring imaginary tea from a tiny teapot.

"Mommy!" she cried; Irene smiled. "Mommy" represented the heavy artillery. She was "Mom" when the circumstances were less urgent.

"Oh, Lisa," said Irene. "I don't know if we have time." But it was only a little past noon; she was stalling while she ran a few calculations in her head. They'd eaten cheese sandwiches from a sack lunch on a bench in the library's courtyard; she'd found good clothes for girls on the discount rack at Brandeis & Sons. The sandals she'd had to pay full price for, but even then she'd come in well under budget. Lisa pulled with both hands at her mother's wrist, dragging her toward the crosswalk.

The recessed entryway to the Astro shone like a cave mouth, glowing with the promise of hidden treasure. Lisa's face lit up in reverent wonder. Irene thought it might be all right to sit in a comfortable seat for a few hours instead of walking around downtown; her feet were tired. There was a woman in a brown dress standing on the sidewalk in front of the theater. As they approached the entryway, Lisa took off at a sprint, unable to resist all the colorful movie posters housed in shining glass. She pointed at one, arm outstretched. "It's cartoons!" she said.

It was Disney's *Bedknobs and Broomsticks*. "This one might be for bigger kids," said Irene, her eyes scanning the five-by-seven lobby cards that framed the poster—a magician with his hands above his head, fire shooting from white-gloved fingertips; a headless ghost floating across a room, trailed by a hat in midair and two disembodied legs walking by themselves; and a strange family portrait, showing three human actors flanked by cartoon animals—two grinning vultures, a bear in a sailor suit, and a lion with a golden crown on its head.

"I'm almost five," Lisa said.

"Four and a half," Irene corrected her.

"Almost five," Lisa said again. She was good with numbers. The heat of the bulbs radiated outward from the ticket booth out front; it felt like she'd entered a dream.

"Are you a churchgoer?" asked the woman from the sidewalk, keeping a respectful distance. Her dress was plain but not frumpy; it had pockets on the front that stood out like Roman numerals on a watch. She offered a tract.

"When I get the chance," said Irene, flashing on memories of her young life in Tama and then smiling, delighted, as she took up the tract: "I have this one! I've read it!" Ahead, Lisa was lost in all the giant movie posters behind glass: *Silent Running. The Cowboys. Conquest of the Planet of the Apes.*

"Oh!" said the woman in the brown dress. "I haven't seen you."

"I got it last winter," she said. "Or just before winter, anyway. A young man"—she caught herself quickly—"a man with a beard gave it to me."

"Michael!" said the woman, her eyes big: "You met Michael!"

"I—yes, I suppose so," said Irene. "Anyway, our church is across the river, where we live."

It seemed to Irene that the woman was looking very deeply into her eyes. It was unusual. "Is your church alive?" she asked in a tone that hinted at uncertainties, unforeseen outcomes, vague worries: concern.

"Oh, there aren't so many of us," she said: she'd taken the question to be about the liveliness of the congregation. "Not everybody makes it in every Sunday." It was true; most Sundays Irene herself just couldn't find the time no matter how she tried. Life seemed so busy.

"Oh," said the woman sadly. "Your church is not alive."

"Well, it's not so bad as all that," said Irene. She brooked so few offenses in her daily life that she wasn't quite sure what to do with this one. She liked the Church of the Redeemer; it made the town feel less small.

"I'm sure it's fine," said the woman, adjusting her tone. She located a stubby pencil in her dress pocket, taking the tract back from Irene and circling something on its reverse in one quick motion before handing it back. "There are a lot of fine churches but time is short now."

Irene tucked it away in the pocket of her cardigan. "If you don't mind my asking, where are you from?" she said, meaning only to make small talk, to steer things into happier terrain: she'd been good at this in her waitressing days.

"Michigan, originally," said the woman. "I'm Lisa."

"That's my daughter's name!" said Irene, pointing over at Lisa, whose face was now pressed up against the glass doors of the the-ater: she could see the popcorn machine inside, yellow light beck-oning above a plush red carpet.

"It's harder when you have children," the woman said. Irene looked again at her eyes: there was something locked away in there, not quite buried.

"That's strange," said Irene; she didn't want to seem stern, but she felt mildly insulted.

"Oh, I have children myself," said the woman, smiling for the first time, deep lines suddenly appearing at the corners of her smile. Irene noticed that she was very beautiful, and wondered why she hadn't seen it earlier. "It just makes life busier, I mean. Harder to find time."

"Mom!" said Lisa, turning.

"We have to go," said Irene.

"Do come to church, if you can, sometime," said Lisa in the brown dress, grown-up Lisa from the church whose name and address had been absent from the tract Michael'd given Irene last fall but whose address—still headless, still without a name—was printed and now circled in dark pencil on the otherwise identical tract now being urged into Irene's hand: just a number and a street in Council Bluffs. In the margin, in pencil, someone had written: *Wed. 10 a.m., Fri–Sun 9:30 a.m.*

"Well, I hope we can, sometime," said Irene, beginning to turn.

"Good luck," said Lisa.

"Mom!" said Lisa Sample, now standing in front of the box office, holding a place for her mother.

In open spaces people begin to think about the world of possibilities, about things that might happen that they couldn't have foreseen: possibly our daughter will grow up to be president, possibly swords will be beaten into plowshares, possibly we will all climb into spaceships and go live on the moon. The substance of things hoped for, an endless open field. But there's another region in that realm, and it's actually the biggest spot on the map: that place in which none of this will happen at all, and everything instead will remain exactly as it is—quiet, unremarkable, well ordered and well lit, just exactly enough of everything for the people within its boundaries. A little drab from the outside, maybe: slow, or plain. But who, outside, will ever see it, or learn the subtleties of its textures, the specific tensions of its warp and weft? You have to get inside to see anything worth seeing, you have to listen long enough to hear the music. Or possibly that's a thing you just tell yourself when it becomes clear you won't be leaving. Sometimes that seems more likely. It's hard to say for sure.

Irene was up before everybody else. She had gone out to the street while it was still dark. Friday dinner had been fine: taco casserole; Lisa and Peter both loved it and said so. Lisa related the story of *Bedknobs and Broomsticks* excitedly for her father, entirely in the present tense, scene by scene: "And then they fly to an island on the flying bed, and they get to meet the King, and play soccer with him. But then they trick him and take the star necklace because they need it for the final spell. So he gets super mad and comes running, but Miss Price turns him into a rabbit and he hops away and they fly back home, but when they get there, the star is gone!" Irene watched Peter while he listened to their daughter, saw how attentive he was. The story of the movie went on until almost bedtime.

Every quiet house is different. Sometimes this one felt like it didn't have enough air in it. She woke up a little after four, her mind wholly awake; it was Saturday. She lay in the dark for as long as she could stand it. She kept seeing the smile on the face of Lisa in the brown dress, Lisa from somewhere in Michigan now standing in front of an aging movie palace in Omaha. Irene was attempting to square that smile with the God talk and the endtimes message-making—there was a through line to draw somewhere, a path, however long and wandering. But there were only the two coordinates. In the quiet of the dark, she considered these as they might appear superimposed on a map of someone else's life: anybody's. Peter's, for example—the traces of fatigue at the corners of his eyes while he listened with visible pleasure to Lisa at the dinner table. The fatigue traced one arc, the pleasure another; they were impossible to hide. Place to place to place. Tama to Crescent. Where was the young woman who'd gone off to Ottumwa Heights College in 1957? Hiding around here somewhere: she has to be. People don't just go missing. She got up, dressed quickly, and slipped out through the front door.

It was very dark; she'd turned on the porch light, but her restlessness extended as far as the steps leading down to the bricked walkway. She had her yellow cardigan on. She loved it even though it made her feel her age: she was thirty-five. Thirty-five is not old, but it can feel old.

She fumbled in her pockets, but there was nothing in them: she'd emptied them into the anything drawer when she got home. *We are called as witnesses*. The horizon began rippling with hints of the earliest blackish purple. There are witnesses to weddings, but also to crimes; it was a word that led to a number of places, she thought. *The world apprehends it not*. She wished Peter harbored a little more natural curiosity about church, just a little interest, but he mainly worried about whether there was enough money: "To keep this whole operation afloat!" he'd said once in his joking manner, never wanting to make anyone worry. But Irene, despite herself, had not been able to forestall a vision of their whole operation as a vessel losing its buoyancy, their modest ranch house sinking into the earth, rain gutters filling with dirt and then breaking away from the frame, the dirt covering all, the house and everybody who lived inside it, the noise and the squall and the panic all resolving into a patch of untilled ground that betrayed no hint of the life that had once gone on above it.

4 Peter wished some moment of clarification might present itself: it was hard, by June, to keep silent about the changes in Irene, about the strain those changes were placing on the house over which she presided. But a man like Peter, in the absence of any immediate crisis, can't feel sure about what might occasion such a moment. His wife was a different person from the one he'd known last summer, or even in early spring: that much was plain. But who, in the privacy and safety of his home, says something like "you've changed" to his wife? Actors in movies talk like that, not people.

She'd begun spending more time at church; but this was not a seismic change, and besides, she took Lisa along with her for Greta Handsaker to dote on in the church nursery. Her baby had grown much too big to just be set down and left alone on a nursery floor, but there were plenty of books to read there, and sometimes other children to play with; if Lisa found herself playing with younger children, she'd try to interest them in Drop a Dragon, a game she'd invented with her mother a little over a year ago. In this game, each player draws one unbroken line—of any color, following any arc, however long and squiggly—until a picture emerges, sometimes vague and evocative, sometimes clear as day. They'd called it Drop a Dragon because the drawing produced from its halting initial playthrough had looked a little like an undulating green dragon; in those days, Lisa, still trying out new ways to speak each day, sometimes appended consonants to words that ended in vowel sounds. "What will we call this picture?" Irene had said, holding it up. "Drop a dragon!" she'd said proudly, pointing. It was a story Peter and Irene liked to recount when they could. Everyone always smiled when they got to the punch line.

But Irene brought Bible study home now. Sometimes she read by candlelight before bed. It struck Peter as an odd affectation, the candle; you keep candles around for when the power goes out. She was probably saving the house a few pennies, though, so what was the harm? She did seem to sing a lot now, more than she ever had. It was a little strange. But she wasn't loud or bizarre, just different. And so he kept his thoughts to himself.

She never preached to the family, and she seldom said much that seemed out of character. Occasionally Peter would make romantic advances at night; she almost always rejected these now, but he attributed this to her practical nature. He was still part-time at work, and there'd been no company-wide raise last year; more children were not in their plans. Of all the small differences only one occasion really stood out, and it was a secret he couldn't tell.

She was in the kitchen washing dishes, her back to the living room, where Peter'd dozed off on the sofa. She was singing quietly to herself. As he rose from sleep, after who knew how long, he heard her, the song drifting in as through a light fog. He'd loved her voice the very first time he'd ever heard it, all the way back at Henry's Drive-In; now he lay listening, motionless, trying to identify the hymn. He expected to find something familiar if he listened hard enough; but the key was minor, the tempo slow; and then the melody dropped away, but the song continued at the same pace and tempo, and he realized she'd been praying—chanting—either petitioning God directly under her breath, or reciting some formulaic prayer he didn't recognize or couldn't make out at this distance.

It had a lilt of its own; not, to Peter, a pleasant one. He didn't know where it came from, and he didn't want to follow it out to where it went. He drifted back into his nap, the way you sometimes fall asleep when there's something on your mind you'd rather not think about. When he woke again, there was pot roast in the oven. You could hear the juices sizzling in the pan. The rich smell filled the house.

Lisa was chalking hopscotch squares on the driveway while her father pushed the lawn mower over the grass. He wore a white undershirt and his summer shorts, black checks over alternating gold and white squares. It was very hot outside, and though he'd kept the blades sharp and the mower oiled, the June grass was thick. Sweat ran into his eyes. He stopped near the driveway to wipe his brow with his hand.

Lisa looked up, hearing his heavy breathing. "Sharon's daddy has a lawn mower that's a car," she said.

"I know he does," said Peter. "It's an antique. Her daddy let me take it for a spin once, back when he first bought it." It was a John Deere Model 110. Everyone in Crescent had stopped by the Lumley place to see it when it was new.

"It sounds like an airplane," said Lisa.

"Sure," said Peter. "They call that 'horsepower.'"

"Can we get one?" Lisa said. "It's super fun. Sharon gets to ride it."

"Can't go wrong with a True Value," said Peter, rattling the push mower by its handles.

"Two people can ride on Sharon's lawn mower!" countered Lisa.

"Maybe Santa will bring us one," said Peter; it was a good line, but he didn't get the rhythm right, because he resented having to hear from his daughter about Chuck Lumley's Model 110, which Chuck had been able to afford because his parents owned preferred stock in the Union Pacific. Lisa looked hurt.

"OK," she said, throwing her piece of chalk at the garage door.

"Oh, honey," he said. He sat down on the driveway next to her. Sweat dripped from his forehead onto the cement. "Sure, we can try and get one sometime. They're just kind of—"

"Expensive," Lisa said, finishing the sentence for him. She had heard this word about a lot of things, starting with Baby Alive and continuing on more recently through Malibu Barbie and color TV.

"Yes, expensive," said her father. "They are expensive." He returned to the lawn. He didn't want to make any promises he wouldn't be able to keep if operations kept shrinking at the stockyard. From the corner of his eye he saw Lisa pout a little more, then retrieve her chalk, finishing the squares she'd been drawing and putting big round numbers inside them. It was hard to believe she could write numbers already. In October she'd be six.

"When's Mommy coming home?" she asked when he was pushing the lawn mower back into the garage.

"She should be home in time to fix dinner," he said. It was half past noon. He gave her a conspiratorial look. "What should we do about lunch?"

"Grilled cheese!" said Lisa.

"Coming right up!" said her father, tipping an imaginary cap to her as he headed in mock hurry toward the house.

Let me ask you a question: What do you see in your head when I tell you that one Sunday, toward the end of June, Irene Sample went to a church in Council Bluffs? Are you seeing a Catholic church with a stoup full of cool water just inside the front door, leading through a pair of huge doors into a great high-ceilinged room full of wooden pews with prie-dieus for kneeling? Something more modest and Midwestern, maybe—a Methodist room with an angled ceiling, wooden beams, plenty of light? Are there candles? Stations of the Cross? Carpeting? Is the organ pipe, or electric? Maybe there's an upright piano instead of an organ, maybe a stylized cross behind the altar: the kind of thing you've been looking at for several minutes before you say, Aha, that's the cross, I get it now. You wonder whether you've happened across a particularly modern congregation, but it's not that: it's just that you'd brought a set of assumptions with you when you came inside, some of which concerned the constancy of the cross. But here, suspended above and to the rear of the chancel, is this massive gnarled thing, made, evidently, of straw or strips of green wood. You can see how puny a human body would look if you tethered one to it with rope or fishing line. You can imagine it creaking and rustling while its captive strains against his bonds: no use.

If you shrink that modern greenwood cross down to the size of a poster, and, instead of suspending it with rigging from the rafters of a large room, nail it to some painted-over drywall behind a lectern in an otherwise undecorated storefront next door to an army surplus store, then you have prepared the room in which Irene Sample attended church services in June 1972, two months after she'd accepted a second copy of a tract she'd initially been given by a man named Michael, who had been scavenging for food in an open garbage can in Omaha.

It was Michael who stood at the lectern now. He was not dressed for church: he looked much as he had that day last November. His tan pants were dirty, his beard untrimmed. His hands looked like they'd been scrubbed with pumice—his palms, when he gestured, showed pink—but there was still plenty of dirt under his nails, which were long. Every member of the small congregation in the folding chairs before him looked better than he did: better dressed, better rested, better fed. There were only seven people in the chairs, plus Irene. The room was bright with sunlight. Lisa was playing in their driveway while her father mowed the lawn; Irene, as far as anyone knew, was out shopping.

Michael's text today was from Luke 17:31. "I want to start with Luke, seventeen and thirty-one," he began; he spoke very slowly with his eyes on the book before him, not looking up. He paused, still with his head down, and remained silent for so long that Irene's mind began to wander out into open space. "Simon," he said after a while, extending his hand awkwardly toward a young man seated near Irene.

Simon got up. As long as he'd been sitting still, Irene hadn't noticed that he smelled, but the movement dislodged the scent; it was strong. He stood and began reading from a well-worn Bible. "'In that day, he that shall be on the housetop, and his stuff in the house, let him not go down to take it away; and he that is in the field, let him likewise not return back.' Thank you, Father," he said, and then sat back down again.

"Thank you, Father," echoed Michael, belatedly, after what proved to be the first of many long silences. "We find the Lord saying the same thing in the book of Matthew. It's a little different there. Matthew . . ." He broke off again.

In the space that opened, Irene remembered a Matthew she'd known pretty well at college—he went by Matt. She felt ashamed, remembering Matt in church, even a church as modest as this one. She tried banishing him from her mind, listening hard and focusing. But in the long quiet Michael left between one thought and the next, Matt found all the room he needed, roaring through in his Plymouth Fury all red and shiny, the upholstery on its back-seats soft and warm.

"Matthew specifies what the worker in the field might go back to his house to get," Michael continued finally. He looked out over the seven in their chairs, and also at Irene, his gaze stopping on each of them as it went. His blue eyes were very bright. "Lisa. Twenty-four, seventeen and eighteen."

It was the woman Irene had visited with in front of the Astro Theater. She, like Michael, looked much as she had on the day Irene had seen her; the same dress, the same simple shoes. "His garment," she replied, looking up from her Bible.

"His garment," said Michael, after a long pause. "Let not him that is in the field, turn back to take his garment." An even greater silence followed; Irene thought about Grace Evangelical. Everyone all dressed up at the holidays. Peter in his suit at Christmas services, just the two of them. Before the wedding, before Lisa, precious Lisa, whose dolls now had conversations about going to the movies. Where had the time gone?

Michael looked pained; he closed his eyes. "Think about the worker in the field," he said, impossibly slowing his rhythm even further, not raising his voice but speaking as if to a friend across a table in a diner late at night. "Think about that worker in the field at midday. How he looks out there after half a day's work, when the hour comes. Sweating. Sunburned. There's a reason why Luke

116

wants us to see this worker in the field, why Matthew says you don't go back for your clothes. It's not just that God doesn't mind if you're dirty," he said.

This time he paused for a full minute, still with his eyes closed, eyebrows knitted together; everyone looked up at him, waiting, trying in private degrees of failure or success to keep their minds focused on the message.

"The dirt's a sign," he said, finally relaxing his face and opening his fiery blue eyes. Their gaze looked over the congregation and at the back wall. They appeared, to Irene, like sapphires.

The freezer in the garage was full of beef: even in frugal times, there were plenty of steaks in the Sample house. Irene retrieved a prepackaged box of four and entered the house through a door that led from the garage directly into the living room. Peter was on the couch, watching a baseball game. He got up when she came in; he wasn't overceremonious about it, but he wasn't ever going to be the sort of person who stayed in his seat when his wife entered the room.

"It's three o'clock," he said. He didn't raise his voice, but there was a pleading note in it. *Tell me something.*

"Sorry I'm so late," she said, smiling earnestly, taking hold of and gently squeezing his hand, slowing but not breaking her stride as she headed for the sink, where she put a stopper in the drain and began running warm water.

"It's three o'clock," he said again. "You left at ten thirty."

"Well, I went to Council Bluffs," she said, taking the steaks from their box: they were vacuum-sealed in plastic. She set them under the running water.

"Well, I know that," he said. "But that was four and a half hours ago."

"I didn't go shopping," she said over her shoulder, addressing him directly; she didn't look down or away. There was more innocence than defiance in her expression. There is no defense against innocence.

"Irene," he said, not knowing how else to respond.

"I found a new church," she said, turning off the water. The sink was half-full. The steaks floated there like fat little boats.

"We didn't know where you were," he said. "I had to make excuses to Lisa."

"Oh, Peter," she said, crossing again to the living room. "Yes, I imagine. I am so sorry. The time just got away from me. I did mean to go to the store, too."

"You left at ten thirty," he said again.

She took a step toward him, so that he'd see her face, all of it: her lips, her eyes, her forehead with its two gradually deepening furrows.

"It's a very different sort of church," she said, again taking hold of his hand and squeezing it, gently, the way you might with a child who doesn't and can't grasp your meaning because he is too young to understand. Several years later, at a Greyhound bus station in Minneapolis in the winter, he remembered this exchange, finally recognizing it as the moment of clarification he'd been hoping for in those then-recent days. It can really get quite cold in Minneapolis in the winter.

5 A while later she began saving food scraps in a little plastic bucket on the kitchen counter. It sat just to the left of the sink. She found the bucket in the garage one day while Peter was at work; it had some oil rags in it, which she took out, laundered, folded, and replaced, neatly stacked, on the shelf where the bucket had been. Peter either didn't notice or didn't mind; a small bucket for food scraps on a counter is the sort of thing that can pass without notice almost anywhere. When he'd been a child, his mother had kept a pail under the sink for potato peelings. She fed them to the chickens.

Peter and Irene Sample had no chickens, of course—I say "of course" even though there's really no reason why they couldn't have. It would have been a thrifty move on Irene's part, to have Peter build her a coop one Sunday: save on eggs, save on meat. But back in Tama her house hadn't been that sort of house, and Peter was unsentimental about his childhood. He didn't miss cleaning up after the chickens.

There is at least one different version of Lisa Sample's story, one where the plastic bucket on the counter in Crescent is indeed for some chickens who live in the backyard, pecking and scratching;

anything left over Irene uses for compost, and the lesson young Lisa takes from the bucket is "waste not, want not." She sees the fat, happy chickens outside and eats their eggs each morning, yolks dark and yellow, almost orange, and she's a smart kid, she makes the connection. She grows up to be a person who dilutes the dish soap several times before buying a new bottle: who cleans the windows with vinegar and old newspaper instead of Windex and a paper towel. She unplugs electrical appliances that aren't in use, and waits until evening to bathe, having learned, from her mother, that over time these small choices add up to real savings, which can be kept on hand in case the day should come when a reserve is needed, when new supplies are scant.

In this version of the story she learns all the same lessons, but not from her mother.

Irene attended services in Council Bluffs again the following Sunday, and on several subsequent Sundays through July. She kept up her Wednesday night Bible study in town for most of the summer. One Wednesday in August she came home early; Peter and Lisa were sitting on the sofa watching *Wild Kingdom* together. She closed the front door behind her with greater force than it needed.

"You're home early," said Peter.

"Daddy! Shh!" said Lisa. On the screen a lioness was stalking an antelope, Marlon Perkins narrating in his deliberate cadence, his voice high and clear.

"You're home early," Peter repeated, stage-whispering. Irene looked distracted, her mind elsewhere; she shook her head once or twice as if to dislodge something caught in her hair.

"I think I have some disagreements with the Wednesday Bible study," she said.

"Mommy!" said Lisa in an admonishing tone. Peter got up; he followed Irene to the kitchen, but continued to whisper.

"You walked out of Bible study over a disagreement?" Peter said. He was trying to picture the scene; there were only three other ladies in the Wednesday night group. You couldn't just sneak out the back as you might in a big church on Sunday.

"Pastor Brian had this passage about the church in Macedonia," she said, a little carefully now, calmer than she'd been when she came through the door. "But I know this verse. Michael's gone over it several times."

"Michael's your Council Bluffs pastor," said Peter, filling in the blanks for himself, making sure he hadn't missed something.

"He's gone over it several times," she repeated, and then she stopped. He saw it happen; he'd seen it a couple of times since June, hardly worth noticing the first time. Just a little tic. But it wasn't like her: to cut off her thought mid-stride, to suddenly seal herself away like a bird who sleeps with its eyes open.

"What's the passage?" he asked.

"It's all right," she said. There were some dishes in the drainer. She started putting them away into their cabinets and drawers.

"Well, it can't be worth fighting with anybody about," he said, playfully, lightly, in the old style from long ago.

"Oh, I didn't fight," she said. She sounded more cheerful now. "I only asked a few questions. I just feel like they don't like my questions."

"But you're home early," he said.

"I did come home a little early, yes. I told them I'd forgotten something." She was finished with the dishes; she went back into the living room and sat down in front of the television next to Lisa. The lioness was resting in dry dirt at the foot of an acacia now, yellow sun setting behind her. Peter stayed behind in the kitchen for a moment, thinking, finding compartments into which he might file his questions where they wouldn't bother anyone until later. But he didn't go back to them later. They were fine right where they were. If, in the future, he found he had need of them, he'd know where to look.

Irene did not go back to Pastor Brian's Bible study the following week. She stayed home and cleaned the kitchen and joined the family in front of the TV. There were two ways to think about this development, and it's hard to blame Peter Sample for picking the easier one, the one that involved a mother wanting to spend time with her family instead of arguing about the Bible at a church down the street. The other possibility seemed improbably dramatic to him. He'd never quit anything in his life. There's no need to make a big fuss just because you disagree with someone; you stay where you are until things improve, and you do what you can to help things along. It goes without saying and you shouldn't have to be told. Adherents to this creed usually adopt it when young, and can barely imagine a world beyond it. As creeds go, it's mild, unpresumptuous, hardly worth repeating. That is its general appeal.

In September he'd wondered but by October he was sure: his wife was losing weight. She'd gained a little over the years, mainly after Lisa was born, but all that was gone now; her clothes looked a little big on her. He'd noticed that she usually skipped Sunday dinner now; she said they served a big lunch after services in Council Bluffs—he pictured a big rec room adjacent to a church, flowers on pink tablecloths over round tables with folding legs. It was possible, he knew, that she'd been losing weight for some time; they were so seldom intimate that he had no occasion to consider her body without staring.

Autumn was coming in cold and bracing this year; he slipped his hand into the sleeve of her nightgown one evening after they'd gone to bed. When he tightened his grip around her shoulder blade he could make out its contour against the pads of his fingers. There'd been muscle in that space the last time he'd embraced her.

He was going to kiss her, but he said: "Are you all right?"

"What do you mean?" she said.

He gripped the shoulder blade again, more playfully. "There used to be more of you," he said; in his tone she could hear him smiling.

"Just getting older," she said. She kissed him, on the lips.

"You're only thirty-five," he said.

"Our bodies change," she said, her voice gently descending to a depth he'd heard it reach only once or twice in their lives together, he wasn't sure when and where. She kissed him again; it was dark; he wondered idly if her eyes were closed, whether she meant this or was only taking grave measures to change the subject, and then he kissed her back.

In the morning, after breakfast, he watched while she cleared their plates, letting his gaze dawdle and stray. She was so pretty; she didn't look as sturdy as she once had, but she would always look strong to him: in the way she pivoted before turning, for example, that carefully calculated grace. Had he not been looking, and had her back not been turned to him, he might have missed the connection. But he watched as she scraped the remnants of his breakfast plate into the scrap bucket—crusts, a few bites of egg white—before starting in on her own, with most of the food still on it. Ham, whole eggs. The ham made a little *flop* sound when it landed. Had it been Lisa, Irene would have reproached her: *You're wasting food.*

She scraped the plate clean with her fork, and fit the lid tightly over the bucket.

I want you to see two things before we go where we have to go. The first is a scene one day in late November out in front of the strip-mall church in Council Bluffs. Some men and women have gathered on the sidewalk—seven of them, all familiar to one another and to us. It's cold by now; a few have old sweaters on, but for the most part these people are underdressed for the weather. The ones in sweaters are sitting. The others stand and pace a little. Inside, it's warmer, but the glass doors are locked; Michael isn't here yet.

A car pulls up; its headlights flood the gathering. Irene gets out and exchanges greetings as she heads around to the passenger side, opens the door, and retrieves the scraps pail. It's been filled and emptied many times since Peter first saw Irene empty her breakfast into it and didn't say anything. Tonight it has the ends of some spinach, and broccoli stalks, and generous potato peelings, and a whole helping of french toast from Saturday's breakfast. It's Sunday. She sets the bucket down on the sidewalk and they all join hands to give thanks, and together they eat.

They have finished all their supper and are sitting again in silence when Michael arrives on foot, trudging slowly across the parking lot, having spent the day who knows where. Everyone lowers their heads as he grows near; he brushes, with twitching fingers, the sleeves of a few congregants as he passes. Then he reaches into the pocket of his grubby gray slacks, takes out some keys, and, unlocking the door, goes in without holding it open behind him. Everyone follows in his wake; they find their seats and, in heavy silence, wait.

The second thing is Peter Sample waking up one morning about a month later expecting breakfast. The house is quiet; Lisa is still asleep. It's a weekday. There's a letter on the table in a sealed envelope: it's a Christmas card from Irene, though Christmas was a few days ago. He opens it up. On the front there's a night sky lit by a single star, immense in the blue darkness, a beacon. Inside the card there's a preprinted greeting, which reads:

> *There's a reason*
> *for the season.*

She's signed it, a little happy face next to her signature: light and easy. That was all.

"Most times they leave a note. They want you to find them," the detective from Omaha said in January, looking over the Christmas card at his desk down at the station while Peter scanned his face for signs of hope or despair. A police radio nearby squelched and *skree*d.

He handed the card back to Peter Sample. "This really isn't much to go on," he said.

6 Peter's demands on life had been, up to this point, extremely modest. He lived in the town where he'd been raised, and was satisfied; when times had grown lean, there was enough in reserve to keep the wolf from the door. His wife had been his partner through the lean times, gardening and sewing and restricting leisure to things that were free—church on Sundays, thrift store shopping, Bible study. He had a beautiful daughter and a steady job and a Chevrolet and a television. These were the things you worked to get; they represented success. He'd made a home like the one his father had made for him to grow up in, embellishing it with his own personal touches: he spent time with his daughter in a way men of his father's generation often hadn't with their own kids, and he liked the way that husbands and wives seemed to talk to each other more now than they had in his parents' time. The house felt warm even when it was drafty. It was a comfortable life. There is much to be said in defense of comfort.

Out in his driveway on the morning of December 29, 1975, he stood in the spot where the car ought to have been. He had a cardigan on over an undershirt; it was too cold to stay out here like this for long, but his body was sending him all kinds of unfamiliar panic signals and he couldn't think straight. Irene hadn't gotten him up for breakfast; it was Lisa who woke him up, running into the bedroom and pushing him with both hands, the way you might roll a log, until he woke up. "Where's Mommy?" she said.

He didn't know. "Church?" he said.

"Church was yesterday!" said Lisa, scowling.

Church was yesterday, he thought in the empty driveway, wondering if the church in Council Bluffs had some special holiday services going on that she'd maybe mentioned while his attention had been elsewhere, special services she'd left for in the quiet cold of the early morning without waking him, without setting anything out for breakfast, with only a note on the dining room table that didn't say she was taking the car and didn't say when she'd be back and gave no indication that anything unusual had happened or was about to happen or would continue happening without interruption in the days to follow.

He didn't know how to tell her parents. He reached for the phone, reflexively by this point, then put it back down: he was still steady enough to imagine what it might feel like to the person on the other end of the line. To have your son-in-law call out of the clear blue sky with news like these. It was unthinkable. But it was also unthinkable *not* to call—what if she stayed missing? They'd want to know why he hadn't called earlier, just to let them know.

He'd been making calls all morning. Patricia Lumley's name was one of several on a sheet of notebook paper taped to the refrigerator with phone numbers next to them in case of emergency; he'd known Chuck Lumley since childhood. Chuck wouldn't know, but his wife might.

But she hadn't heard anything, though she sensed, immediately, the discord of the moment. Irene Sample's husband calling, not to talk to Chuck, but to *her*, on a Monday morning, asking whether Irene was over there for some reason. It didn't add up.

"Gee, I don't know," she said when Peter asked the next question, the obvious one: Did she know where Irene might be, what might have happened, did she know anybody else he might call. "Do you want me to look after Lisa today? Sharon's not doing anything."

Sharon was sitting on a pillow on the living room floor, watching game shows on TV. Everyone was ready for winter break to be over. "Tell her to bring Gold Medal Barbie!" she yelled without looking away from the screen.

"Bring her on over," Patricia Lumley said. "It's no trouble, really."

But all the stray signals searching for ground inside Peter's chest found it now. He'd called the wrong person. There was no right person to call. No matter who he called, it was going to get to this point fairly quickly every time, and then they'd know. There wouldn't be any way around it. Best to just get it over with.

"She took the car," he said, his voice catching.

Patricia cupped her hand over the mouthpiece before she raised her voice. "Sharon, get your shoes and coat on!" she said.

Peter was quiet. An unwelcome clarity was settling in.

"We'll be over in a minute," Patricia said.

In any case it was the Coltons, not Peter and Lisa, who received the letter from Irene: the one that came about two weeks later and began *This will be the only time you hear from me.* They called right away. They were very worried, and they wanted to be told what to do, but it was clear from the way Harold Colton's sentences kept trailing off into nothing that he was out of his depth: that he didn't know what to make of it, out of any of it.

"She says she's being taken care of," said Harold on the phone. "What does she mean?" Pressing the earpiece against his temple in Crescent, Peter patrolled the space between question and answer, watching for silence and trying to shore up the gap. Nearby, on the floor, Lisa was playing Drop a Dragon alone. In the one-player version you finish the lines yourself, still trading out crayons to make a colorful dragon.

"Well, I intend to find out," he said weakly. Irene's letter hadn't really left any place for questions about what she meant. She had gone to await the coming of the Most High with His people. The Lord who sees in secret will reward you. She knew they would all meet again.

"Well, I can't figure how you're going to find out unless you can ask her directly," said Harold without a trace of malice: it just seemed to him like something worth bearing in mind.

"I just can't understand it," said Peter.

"Well, I can't either," said Harold, this being the absolute best he could do, given the circumstances.

"I'll call tomorrow," said Peter.

"Yes, please do," Harold Colton said from the old house in Tama where Irene had once lived as a child.

It had taken Michael Christopher six months to groom Irene for departure; there was some question about whether the preacher's last name was Christopher or Christophersen, but Christopher seemed to be the consensus after calling around to various churches in Council Bluffs and Omaha. The storefront next to the army surplus had been abandoned: there was a vase of sad flowers on a folding table near the lectern when the landlord opened the door for Peter and they both walked in. The folding chairs were still set up in rows. The cross on the wall was gone, though Peter'd never known it was there and the landlord hadn't taken any note of it; it was an unrecordable absence. "His rent's current," said the landlord, keys to the place still in hand. "They might still show up one Sunday."

But Peter looked around the room: all the life had gone out of it. This landlord was only putting a good face on things, trying not to say what was obvious. It made no difference to him either way: the rent was paid up. But to Peter it meant several things, if services weren't being held here anymore, if the congregation was truly gone.

In the weeks since she'd gone missing, he'd taken a leave of absence from work: he stayed home with Lisa, calling everyone he could think to call, asking if they'd heard from Irene. He called the local police of every nearby town, alerting them to the existence of the missing-person report he'd filed on the third day of her absence. Then he'd called them all again, one by one, to remind them: first on the next day, and thereafter at least twice a week.

Pastor Brian at Church of the Redeemer told him what little he knew about the Michael Christopher group ("I heard about a traveling preacher, but they get those types coming through Omaha all year. This one brought his church with him, I guess. They all dressed more or less the same. Like ragamuffins"), and he tried to give comfort, to be helpful. He passed along a few names, pastors from bigger churches in Council Bluffs or Omaha. "They'd know better than I would, I guess," he said, shaking Peter's hand at the church office's door. "I know Irene loves the Lord. She knows the Lord's plan for her life is with her family, I just know it."

"She loves coming here," said Peter. He'd slept badly every night since first waking up alone.

"Well, now," said the pastor. "There's got to be a good answer to this. Everyone here is praying for her."

"I don't know what I'm supposed to do," said Peter.

"We have to be patient, especially when it's hard to be patient," said Pastor Brian. "I know the answer will come in time."

"I don't—" Peter stopped. The thought was terminal, inconsequential. There wasn't anything on the other side of it. "I don't know what I'm supposed to do."

The school in Crescent was very small and when the children came back after winter break everybody knew. Peter walked in with Lisa and called Mrs. Rethmeier aside on the first day back. "Most of them probably know already," he said. She nodded sympathetically. There was no one in town who didn't know about Irene Sample by now. Everybody had an opinion.

At school that day and through the weeks that followed, Mary Rethmeier kept an unobtrusive eye on Lisa; she'd been a teacher for many years and knew how to watch without being seen. At recess, everything seemed fine: Lisa and Sharon and Gail and Liz all jumped rope together in the auditorium, or, after the snow had melted, swung from the jungle gym bars out on the playground. Lisa did not look like a little girl whose mother had suddenly disappeared just after Christmas, and of whom no trace had been seen since.

In class she seemed distracted. She began to draw in the margins of her addition notebook, lines connecting to one another in different colors, suggestive of shapes but never fully relaxing into a single picture. The line segments followed one another out into the middle of the page: chain links and spirals morphing gradually into kidney or heart shapes, ballooning. Between segments she traded crayons, alternating colors, crossing the page from right to left and back again and then looping around to the reverse, dropping dragons over both sides of the paper until they covered the entire assignment.

If you work with or around children, you often hear a lot about how resilient they are. It's true; I've met children who've been through things that would drive most adults to the brink. They look and act, most of the time, like any other children. In this sense— that they don't succumb to despair, that they don't demand a space for their pain—it's very true that children are resilient.

But resiliency only means that a thing retains its shape. That it doesn't break, or lose its ability to function. It doesn't mean a child forgets the time she shared in the backyard with her mother gardening, or the fun they had together watching *Bedknobs and Broomsticks* at the Astro. It just means she learns to bear it. The mechanism that allowed Lisa Sample to keep her head above water in the wake of her mother's departure has not been described or cataloged by scientists. It's efficient, and flexible, and probably transferable from one person to another should they catch the scent on each other. But the rest of the details about it aren't observable from the outside. You have to be closer than you really want to get to see how it works.

PART THREE

✳

1 "Oh, my God," Sarah Jane said when she answered the knock at Lisa Sample's door. Jeremy was standing on the porch looking dazed. His shirt was covered with blood.

"Sorry," he said reflexively.

"No, no," she said. She put her arm over his shoulder and led him inside. "Are you all right?"

"It's not me, it's Ezra."

"Oh, my God," she said again. "Where is he? Where is he?"

Jeremy turned halfway back toward the door he'd just come through and nodded stiffly in the direction of the highway. "Paramedics," he said. "I didn't know where else to go."

Sarah Jane grabbed a remote from an end table and turned off the television in the living room. "Didn't they offer you a ride?" she asked, trying not to sound irritated; in the absence of details she'd begun stitching a story together, something that would explain both why Jeremy'd happened to set out for Collins and how he'd done so just in time to find Ezra in the road, his errand interrupted, the remnants of its purpose surrounding the wreck in broken plastic pieces and shiny lengths of unspooling tape.

"Could I get a little water," he said.

"Oh, my God, of course," she said, hurrying to the kitchen.

"Could I use the restroom," he called after her.

"Just through the door on the other side of the couch," she said from the kitchen over the sound of the cooling water rushing from the tap.

Washing Ezra's blood off his hands and face in Sarah Jane's bathroom, trying to listen to his thoughts over the new ringing sound in his ears alongside the rhythmic *whoosh* of his own pulse: Did she live here now? Was that it? It was obvious she'd been spending a lot of her time out here, but he hadn't given much thought to the technicalities. Nobody likes a nosy neighbor. In the mirror, he saw his face looking tired, like he'd been up all night worrying, dusty sweat encrusting at his temples. It was a little past four in the afternoon.

Back in the living room she was waiting with a glass of ice water. "Rest," she said, patting the couch cushion a respectful half-arm's length from where she sat.

"Thanks," he said. The coldness of the glass in his hand drew him earthward, down into the present moment, then eased him further down; he might easily have nodded off to sleep, glass still in hand, like an old man in a rest home. All the chaos of the highway began to ebb, seeking the place where dreams go after you wake up: the sirens breaking the stark silence; the paramedics emerging from the van all at once, two-way radios squelching arhythmically; the team strapping Ezra to the stretcher while the driver asked Jeremy question after question in rapid succession. How long has he been unconscious? Do you have any idea what he hit? Do you have a phone number for his family?

"What happened to Ezra?" she said.

"I guess he flipped that old Citation," said Jeremy. "I don't know why he drives that thing. Anyhow, it was upside down in the ditch."

"Gosh," she said. The blood on his shirt was still wet and gummy; she didn't want to ask the obvious question.

"He was breathing when I picked him up. Unconscious, though. Thrown from the car, I guess. I figured I should just get him out of the road."

"Sure."

Jeremy's momentum had been arrested; he didn't know what to do for conversation now. It didn't seem like a good time to put in notice anymore. "You know those telephone pole call boxes?" he said instead. "The telephones inside are like antiques. I had to say everything two or three times before they got the message."

"Oh, jeez," she said.

"Yeah. I think they usually have some waterproof metal door, but this one didn't even have any door."

"Oh, jeez," she said again, and then, reasoning that she'd waited long enough: "Why—what was he doing all the way out here?"

Jeremy felt the adrenaline letdown take hold, his body sinking into the soft couch. It was so comfortable. He looked up at her until he caught her eyes, and then held her gaze just long enough to convey, as gently as he could, that he didn't consider her question a real question. A person like Ezra wouldn't have been on his way to Collins unless somebody'd called him there on some business, on or off the books.

"We should probably go get all those tapes off the road. Might rain," he said after it had been quiet for a minute or so.

She rose rather quickly to her feet.

"No real hurry, though," he said, smiling a little, rubbing his eyes while holding his face in his hands, really pressing the pads of his fingers down hard into his eyeballs: the pressure felt good, incredible really. "That car's not going anyplace."

Sarah Jane was at the hall closet, taking down a couple of canvas totes from a hook.

"You're right, though, it might rain," she said.

She stood by the wreck with her hand over her mouth for a minute or more; the hypnotic uniformity of rural highways allows for plenty of cars in ditches, but Ezra's crash had been especially dramatic. There were long skid lines on the blacktop, and the driver's-side door had been torn from its hinges. It lay interior-side-up thirty feet from the wreck, its window shattered.

When the shock ebbed a little, she started picking up tapes from the highway; there were dozens. She put them one at a time into a tote bag until it was full, then carried it back to her car and traded it out for an empty one. Jeremy scowled as he helped her scour the highway and the shoulder, but didn't say anything. He wouldn't have known where to begin.

"They're just—they're *everywhere*," she said at one point, her voice the only sound for miles.

When she'd recovered as many as she could find, and then spent ten fruitless minutes searching for more, she stood for a moment at the roadside, sizing up what remained of Ezra's old Citation. It was upside down; she could have crawled in through the missing door and scoured the interior, but there was no way of checking the trunk.

"Better get going," she said with audible reluctance.

"I guess," said Jeremy. "We should maybe call the hospital."

"Here," she said, retrieving a cell phone from her pocket. "There's no phone back at the house."

He accepted it while fixing her with a harder look than he liked having to give anybody, because he'd already seen the army-green rotary phone attached to the wall of the kitchen, and he knew the telephone wires running all down State Highway 65 weren't just there for show.

"It says there's no service," he said, holding the phone at arm's length with the screen facing away from him so she could see it. In the future, cell phones like the one Sarah Jane handed Jeremy would be referred to as "burners": cheap phones, often purchased without a contract at a department store, to be used for a very short period of time and then thrown away.

"Should we check a little farther down the road?" she said.

"You have to let me use your phone," he said, knowing what he had to say next, resenting it. "I saw it, it's right there in the kitchen."

She stared blankly past him, as if there were a figure emerging from the fields across the highway, and drew in a deep, even breath through her nostrils, trying not to let it show.

"Of course it is," she said at last, not meeting his gaze. "What am I thinking, of course there is, let's just go."

It was a mile and three quarters back to the Collins house; the rain started up after a minute or so. If it rains, and you've been worrying out loud about whether it might rain later, then that's a good omen. The corners of Sarah Jane's mouth turned up slightly, involuntarily.

To Jeremy she looked ominous; this morning had been awful. "It's none of my business," he said, finally, against the grain of a lifetime of social conditioning, "but why are you—you know—your house is back in Nevada, do you even live there any more, I don't know." He had done his best not to make it sound like he was prying. Still, he looked over at her from the passenger's side, checking her face for clues.

When she spoke, it seemed clear she'd practiced her response. "I met a friend who needs a little help," she said, her eyes never leaving the road.

"All right, but Ezra—"

There were no cars coming from either direction. Even the smallest breezes breach the quiet a little on these roads away from town.

"He's just a kid."

Her expression did not change. "My friend needs all the help she can get," she said lightly, as if it were something already asked and answered. It takes a crew to raise a building. Everyone needs a little help sometimes.

It would be great to tell you that you're going to see Irene Sample again—that we've shifted our focus in order to make her return all the more joyous and conflicted, that she's going to call Collins from someplace far away, maybe today, and say she's all right, that her life has been a journey through good times and bad; that she'll say "I can't explain it, I can hardly believe it myself" while her daughter, grown now, sobs aloud, stifling her cries with her free hand, finally calming herself enough to tell her aged mother to come visit, come visit, she'll pay for the ticket, she'll drive up to get her if she has to: Where is she? It would be my sad duty then to tell you about how the line goes dead as Lisa is unburdening herself, the dial tone breaking in to alert her that for some indeterminate stretch of time she has been talking to herself, or to no one, or to the birds in the field she sees through the window from her place by the wall phone in the kitchen. I wouldn't like that—following Lisa out onto the front porch where the gourd bird feeder colonized by wasps is now gone, replaced by a hummingbird feeder—which is tidier, sure, but birds nest in the gourds, they lay eggs that hatch, it's wondrous. And what does she say to Jeremy and Sarah Jane when they return from surveying the scene of the accident? How can she explain?

I'd settle for saying that Irene just shows up one day a few weeks from now out of the clear blue sky, the way people sometimes seem to do in Lisa's life. There she is now—an old woman, pulling up in an Oldsmobile Cutlass Ciera, tires pleasantly crushing the stray unrenewed clumps of gravel along the long driveway. It's summer, she's wearing sunglasses. Sarah Jane hears the car drive up, hears the driver kill the motor: Lisa, who's that? *It's my mother. She's found me.*

It'd even be OK if we had to learn that something has gone terribly wrong—that she gets arrested for shoplifting in Rapid City one year and takes a plea, and when the group moves on, they leave her behind; and so, after serving her thirty days in the county jail, she emerges directionless, no sense of where to go, afraid to see if the bridges she crossed to get here are still standing: and so she walks until she finds a church, Assemblies of God Rapid City, and they find a parishioner who's willing to give her room and board until she can get back up on her feet; and then she calls home to Crescent, but the number's been disconnected, because Peter and Lisa don't live there any more. They left ages ago. They are driving around the country looking for Irene, following up on tips and rumors that never pan out. Lisa's childhood is ruined; Peter can't put himself back together; Irene can only guess at this from the message she's hearing, *The number you have called is not in service at this time*, but her guess is good enough. She can't call her parents; she can't stand it; there is the possibility that they are both dead. It's been seven years. She finds work at a drugstore, abandoned by the family she's forsaken her husband and daughter for.

She sleeps as long as she can at night. Just being awake feels hard most days. She tries to read her dog-eared Bible, but the connection is lost. She buries her memories under any worthless dirt she can find to pile on top of them: watching television, doing crosswords, working jigsaw puzzles from the Goodwill on a coffee table in her efficiency apartment.

None of this is true, or maybe some of it is. I don't know. Irene Sample was never seen again. Several private detectives reported leads and rumors to Peter until his money ran out; once, Patricia Lumley saw a woman standing in the alley behind the post office and thought it was Irene, but she didn't get out of her car to check. It could have been anybody, she told herself when she got home: and besides, wouldn't Irene be much older by now? Of course she would. It had been years.

2   He nodded goodbye at Sarah Jane while backing down the long driveway, in what felt like the first moment of real substance since leaving the house that morning; everything from then to now had already begun to seem like a weightless vision. The exhilaration of the highway out from town; the blunt trauma of the flipped Citation in the ditch with Ezra's unconscious body out in front of it; the dream of arrival at the Sample house, the return to the site of the crash: they all folded rapidly into one another, light fading down and back up between individual moments in a hurried preview of the familiar scene now growing smaller and more concentrated on the other side of the windshield. The cornfield to the left, that work shed at its edge. The empty driveway in the sun. The house down at the end. It all looked different with light on it, but there could be no doubt. He had seen it before.

The fuel indicator was nearly red by the time he got back to Story County. He pulled off the highway at a Casey's in Colo to get gas; at the counter, paying, he saw the foil-wrapped hamburgers under the bright heat lamp, all that shiny false promise. He knew they would be dry, bland, barely worth eating, but he was suddenly ravenous. The huge bites he tore off with his teeth as he drove, burger in one hand and steering wheel in the other, felt like the most nourishing food he'd ever eaten, like something from the potluck at a wake. The point isn't how healthy the food is, he thought to himself, crumpling the sad silver wrapper. The point is how hungry you are.

His father hadn't come home from work yet. Jeremy went back to his bedroom, taking his shirt off and tossing it into a corner of the room as he entered. He felt like calling Stephanie to tell her what he'd learned; he imagined her excited voice on the other end, making plans for the next move, sorting through possibilities. It might restore a little light to the scene, breathe some air into it. But he wanted to lie down first, just for a minute; and, of course, as soon as he did, his body began to feel heavy, like an old tree. His thoughts grew less coherent, following an instinctive pattern of connection and reference as he drifted into a deep sleep—gathering, as he went, images of Stephanie's maps and printouts, blue ink fresh on the paper spread out across the table at Gregory's, brighter days of the fairly recent past.

"Where do you get them all?" Sarah Jane said. They were in the cellar; Lisa was hunched over an editing block at a worktable, razor in hand. She felt afraid asking; if their conversations approached this subject, it was only to circle it from a place high above, like a flock of starlings shading a field.

"Get what," she said.

"The tapes," Sarah Jane said, not impatiently. Lisa at her work was someone you might think you envied: her focus clear and steady, somehow removed from the object of its scrutiny. There were only the motions of the work, their total care, her steady hands.

"Some you make yourself," she said, not looking up, "and some you already had."

Sarah Jane laughed a small laugh. "'You'?"

Lisa turned now to look over her shoulder; she, too, was smiling. "You know what I mean. Besides, who knows?" She reached for a tape atop a five-high stack, held it up: it was unlabeled. It might have been blank, but it could have been anything. "There's so many of them now. Some of these could have been made by anybody."

She turned back to the table to resume her cuts and splices; Sarah Jane could see the yellow grease pencil on the loose lengths of master tape. It was easier than she might have guessed, regarding the process while trying not to dwell on its ends. She didn't like to think of the tapes shot on the property, the ones with identifiable signposts. But these others seemed benign. By themselves they were nothing: long static shots. It was kind of neat how different they felt when Lisa got done with them.

"But you made most of them," she said, the dread returning, not meaning to be rude but wanting to help as much as she could.

"A fair number of them, yes," Lisa said, again without looking up, absorbed in her labor. The soft spots in her armor were hard to see, but you meet a lot of lonely people working the counter at a video store. You wish you could do something for them. There might be some mutual benefit in it, who knows, if there were only some readily available point of contact.

There was no reason to press the point. She watched Lisa's fingers nimbly working at the plastic sprockets and hinges, the warm quiet of the cellar returning. "Is there a specific word for the little thing you push in to make the housing open?" she asked when the moment had passed.

"The release lever," Lisa said. "I used to have a printout of the schematic right on this wall."

———

Even if you're all grown up, the sound of a parent's voice calling you awake from sleep can make you feel like a child—like there's somebody who wants to make sure all's well with you, who cares enough to ask.

It wasn't dark yet—the days were getting longer—but it wouldn't be long. Steve's voice was gentle, coming in through the haze: "Hey, big man. Hey, big man."

Jeremy opened his eyes but stayed put for the moment. "How long was I out," he said.

Steve chuckled. "Well, I wasn't here when you went down for your nap," he said.

Jeremy sat up. "Nap," he repeated, also laughing.

Steve spotted the shirt on the floor and saw the deep stain on the front. "Everything OK?" he said.

"It's real bad," Jeremy said, opening his dresser, grabbing the first shirt his hand landed on: *Cyclones '98*. "Ezra went into a—his car went off the road."

Steve's eyes grew wide. "Where?"

"In Collins. Well, near Collins," Jeremy corrected himself. "He's in the hospital now. We called—he's stable now, they say."

"Who called?"

"Me and Sarah Jane."

Steve looked like a schoolboy learning long division, trying to hold too many figures in his head. "Did she see the accident?" He'd reached the end of the obvious questions, but his need to know more was feral: by the time the paramedics pulled Linda from the ditch, she'd been there for hours, no witnesses to the crash, no way of knowing what her last moments had been like and only the pathologist's estimation of when they'd finally come to pass.

"No, nothing like that," Jeremy said. "She stays out in Collins sometimes, she was at her friend's house when it happened."

146

Steve took a quick measurement of the expression on his son's face: he could see that there was more to know. But he knew his own limits. Once an overturned car came into the picture he had only so much time to get onto a different subject before his mind would start wandering to places best avoided. But Jeremy caught him looking, and then it was too late.

"It wasn't like Mom's, Dad," Jeremy said. "He was out in front of the car when I found him. I think he went through the windshield. But there wasn't—"

"Nothing on top of him," Steve said, finishing the thought: no point in shrinking from it now. "OK. Thanks. You going to go to the hospital?"

"Maybe tomorrow," said Jeremy. "Give the family a little time."

"Good thinking," said Steve.

"Guess I'll get a shower," said Jeremy, stretching.

"Fine," said Steve, and then, impulsively, clumsily, worried that there wouldn't be a better opportunity to say it: "Hey, big man: if it's all right, I don't want Shauna to know about any of this."

Jeremy scratched the back of his head with both hands, head down. "Of course not," he said. "She coming over?"

Steve blinked. "Not tonight, no."

Afternoon light traced the shape of a sugar maple onto the carpet; the tree'd been there for as long as Jeremy could remember. Once, as a child, he'd asked his dad how old it was. "Who knows?" Steve had replied cheerfully from his station at the Weber, flipping a burger and admiring the fresh black grill marks on it. "Older than anybody here, anyway!"

"It's all right," Jeremy said after a minute, with a tenderness beyond his years. His father was still standing in the doorway, visibly waiting for some kind of reply. "I know what you mean."

147

The northbound lane is closed now. Fat orange barrels scroll past the passenger's-side window, bobbing into view like buoys on a lake. It isn't clear what kind of work the road needs over there on the other side of the cones; it looks fine, and there aren't any workers around. At one point a parked steel drum compactor breaks the spell, but there's nobody up top.

A low table with some back issues of *Family Circle* on it, and a modest sofa, and an old recliner, and the television resting on a cabinet originally meant for storing plateware. Lisa and Sarah Jane sitting together, visiting in the bluish light of the screen.

"Why are you letting me move in?" said Sarah Jane. "It's kind of strange, if you think about it."

"You look tired," said Lisa.

"It's a pretty—" She looked for a word that wouldn't sound like she was complaining. "It's a pretty generous thing to offer somebody just because they look tired," she said.

"It's not a big deal. You're not the first person to come and stay here for a while."

She had suspected this fish was down there in the depths somewhere, but it was a surprise to see it flop up onto the deck like that.

"Where'd the others go," she said.

"They're fine."

"What do you mean, they're fine."

"They're all just fine."

"Where are they, though."

Lisa waved her hand toward the big window.

"They're out there somewhere," she said.

"You knew them, though."

"Of course I knew them, they were here."

"Isn't that them?" Here nodding toward the TV.

Here laughing: "No, no. Those are just people in transition."

"But you know who they are."

"Maybe. I think. Mainly in a general sense."

"In a general sense."

"Loosely. Generally who they are, were. At any rate they've moved on."

"You mean they're all dead."

"Maybe. I guess. I don't really know. They're people who were here once. I'm their witness. I keep their memory alive."

"I don't get it," said Sarah Jane.

"Sure you do," said Lisa. "Everybody does."

"Everybody what?"

Lisa rose to her feet, took a deep breath, and shook her hair. It was late and the moon was so bright you could see it through the drawn blinds.

"Everybody leaves a little something behind," she said, heading up the stairs. "I'll see you in the morning."

She lay awake later, thinking: *Keep their memory alive.* People you once knew who've gone somewhere: those memories everyone can understand. They are hothouse flowers. You tend to them because the world will be diminished by their loss. But the memories to which *Shed #4* and *Farrowing Crate* bore witness—whose were those? They were nothing, they went nowhere. No names, half-seen faces, no locatable beginnings or ends.

But there was the one scene, though, that *did* feel like an end, the last one on the tape labeled *State Road.* That woman running down the driveway, her hair seen free for the first time. Someone following. The sound of cold gravel underfoot, the cold readily established by clouds of steam emerging from a panting mouth at lens-height behind the camera, fogging the screen as we pursue our quarry out toward the road. Sarah Jane couldn't fix the outline definitively, couldn't say why this felt like the one scene after which no other could be envisioned. But in the hidden recesses of her heart, at the bottom of a diagram she'd never looked at under good light, that's what it was: the concluding moment, the nearest thing to a climax these dozens of tapes had to offer. The opening out onto the blacktop. The last blurred burst of information before the transmissions stopped coming forever.

3   Sometime after dinner that evening, as the washing machine in the garage chugged cheerfully away, cleaning the blood out of Jeremy's clothes, Steve dug his journal out from the back of the drawer where it had lain unattended for years. He turned to the point where he'd left off; that final entry before the long break ventured so far out into the depths: it had felt like a purging, and it was. He'd seldom thought of the journal at all after writing it. It had taken him over a year, back then, to get to the place where he could open himself up to say *It feels dark a lot of the time.* This new entry took the shortcut.

Linda I think Jeremy's hurt or in trouble and I don't know what to do, it says. *I can't lost Jeremy. Help me Linda I don't know what to do.*

Ken Wahl never saw this entry, and neither did anybody else. After writing it, not stopping to correct *lost* for *lose,* Steve tucked it back underneath the dress socks he never wore. Then he went out to the kitchen to clean up. They'd had chicken alfredo with noodles. By now he could make it without having to read the instructions on the jar. He turned to chicken alfredo when he wanted to feel secure.

———

Jeremy was awake and restless by midnight. Turning in early had thrown him off. Shifting and turning in bed, he tried unsuccessfully to calm his mind. After a while he gave up.

"Hey, it's Jeremy," he said quietly into the mouthpiece, standing in the living room at the wall phone in the dark, wearing the same basketball shorts and undershirt he'd used as pajamas since high school.

"It's twelve thirty," Stephanie said. She'd been sleeping.

"Oh," he said. For him it was still yesterday, all that blood and sun and glass: for her it was only the middle of the night. "Sorry."

"It's OK. What is it?"

"I—" Where was he going to start? "You were right about Collins."

"Collins?"

"The house." Nothing. "The one from the movies."

In some places night gets louder in the summertime. Cicadas were buzzing outside, choral, alien. He looked out at the backyard from where he stood, hearing their sound but seeing no motion, just hearing the drone. They attached themselves to trees and sang all summer. When it got cold they'd be gone.

"No, listen," she said after a long silence, stirring finally free from sleep. "I decided you were right. You know? *You* were right."

"I was right?"

"It's none of our business."

"I didn't say that," he said.

"You said, 'I don't want to know.'"

"That's right," he said. "I didn't want to know, but I had to go out to Collins to talk to Sarah Jane, and I—"

"Sarah Jane lives *here*," said Stephanie. "She's right down the street."

"Well, but no, she doesn't. She drives in from Collins most days now, when she comes in at all."

Stephanie laughed. "This is new," she said.

"Yeah, I don't know," said Jeremy. "She seems kind of worried when she comes in."

Stephanie was now sitting upright in bed. The San Francisco job was beginning to look like a dead end. She still wasn't sure how much longer she could really stand Nevada, but when Jeremy'd refused to go adventuring down the county roads, she'd taken it to heart: she wanted adventure, but she didn't want it to get messy. But it seemed like now it was messy already, and Jeremy was less than a mile away.

"Oh," she said.

Jeremy felt himself getting ready to do something he wasn't comfortable doing.

"She's a nice person. I can't figure it out. I have to talk to some-body about this," he said.

He couldn't see her smiling in the dark, and she calibrated her tone so he wouldn't be able to hear it, either. "Do you want to come over?" she said.

At one thirty a.m. in Nevada at the very end of spring, his was the only car driving evenly down the side streets, turning cautiously, not even attracting imaginary attention. Jeremy reflected upon the moment as best he could, situated as he was, there at its center. It felt quietly dramatic, inward-turning: an unfamiliar feeling. He settled into it. There was no telling how long it would last.

"I still have the charts," she said. She was at the closet door, in her bedroom, still in her nightclothes: Cyclone Red sweatpants and an oversized Lake Okoboji T-shirt. In a previous lifetime, last winter, this would have made Jeremy feel profoundly uncomfortable, but the events of the day had left him open to unfamiliar positions.

Stephanie's apartment was just off downtown, on the second floor of a three-story building that predated the Second World War. Steve and Jeremy lived in a ranch home that had gone up at the same time as the rest of the ones surrounding it; at Stephanie's, he felt acutely conscious of how little he actually knew about other people's lives, and of several assumptions he'd always carried but never named. You could see the whole of the place as soon as you came in through the front door; there was a fern on a single bookcase, and another hanging from a hook in the window frame, and not much else. Her bed was right in the middle of the room with a collapsible table next to it, like the ones in hospitals. The window looked out onto Sixth Street; he kept stealing glances at the sidewalk below.

Her charts consisted of two notebooks and a large sheet of paper from an artist's sketch pad with an actual map drawn on it: cut sections from laser printouts were affixed to its edges by paper clips. It was big enough to hang on the wall; its four corners bore faded tape marks.

"I was really mad at you," she said, not looking up from her work.

"I know," he said, also keeping his gaze downward, following her hands as they smoothed out rumpled papers and tried to settle on a definitive arrangement, keen to keep up as much of his guard as he could readily access without being obvious about it.

In the future, would he spend as much time in the car every day as he had today? Once you get outside of town after dark you can't see much through the windows: the night's still dark and big off the shoulders of the Iowa highways. He was riding out to Collins, too tired to drive his own car, thoughts pleasantly sloshing around inside his head like slurry in a cement mixer. Stephanie drove a 1981 Thunderbird she'd been given by her grandmother; it got eleven miles to the gallon and sailed across the asphalt like a ship.

"What if they're still awake?" she said without looking over at him.

"It's three in the morning," he said, and then, looking at the clock in the dashboard and correcting himself: "It's three thirty. Farmers might get up pretty soon but Sarah Jane's no farmer."

"I thought you said they had pigs."

"No," he said, a little dreamily, picturing what the place would look and smell like if there were even a couple of hogs on the plot. Imagining the different feel as he ascended the porch steps earlier that day, his shirt wet with Ezra's blood.

"Don't know where I got that, then," she said, smiling.

Jeremy leaned back against the window, stretching his left leg out a little on the bench seat.

"Thanks for doing this," he said. "I feel all backwards."

"I think you kind of like the excitement," she said. "Can you at least admit you kind of like it?"

"We'll see if I do," he said, gently closing his eyes, completely adrift for possibly the first time in his life, hoping that the jolts of fear that kept flashing up through his fatigue weren't visible on his face.

What were they expecting: floodlights? High-wattage motion-sensitive lamps that come on with a pop when the car gets within range of the beam? There's no light at all. The waning moon is visible, but weak; the stars are dazzling, but strictly decorative, useful only for calculating calendar time. Once she's killed the headlights, midway through her left turn into the driveway, at Jeremy's urging—he was nearly whispering: "Now, now. Before they hit the living room windows"—everything goes dark.

The voice came from the porch before they were even fully out of the car.

"What are you doing here?" said Lisa Sample, still not visible from where Jeremy and Stephanie stood.

He quickly put on his disguise, the one he'd been born with, that made him look and sound like a man on the other side of middle age who didn't have any use for conversation. "Worried about Ezra," he said.

Behind Lisa, the blue glow of a television throbbed and ebbed against the living room window from the inside.

"Watch your step," she said, pointing at the stairs leading up to the porch.

4   "Can you go out to Grimes and show Lyle how to operate the Super Boom?" Bill was saying. Jeremy was at the table saw cross-cutting wood. It was busywork; most clients who needed wood in bulk could do the cutting themselves. But he'd learned in his first winter at Veatch & Son that he liked to keep his hands busy when it got quiet around the yard. There was always at least one person on a weekend coming in wanting odd lengths of wood for some project or another, so it wasn't an entirely idle effort. It beat just standing around.

"Lyle," said Jeremy, not laughing but almost. Lyle was almost seventy years old, and it was time for him to stop farming, but he was third generation. He had a lot of money; he'd held onto every square foot his father handed down to him. Now he rented most of it out, but on the five acres behind his house he farmed—sweet corn, squash, beans. He kept right on buying new equipment every year, but most of it just upgraded things he'd bought the year before. The Super Boom was a mystery—it was a skid steer, something you used on construction sites to move huge piles of dirt from one place to another. The only thing Jeremy could imagine Lyle needing a skid steer for was plowing snow; it was only September, and besides, it was inconceivable that he didn't already have several machines that'd do the job.

"I don't know, either," said Bill. "I'm kind of curious."

"There's really not much to it," Jeremy said out at Lyle's farm, climbing into the cab. "You already have a Bobcat; it's pretty much the same deal."

Lyle peered in and made a show of looking around, but there isn't a whole lot to see inside the cab of a skid steer. "Handles are a little different," he said.

"That's the joystick control," said Jeremy. "It's electronic, but it shouldn't give you any trouble." He put the bucket through some motions.

"That's what I thought, but it started jerking all around when I started it up," said Lyle.

Jeremy climbed down. "Oh, yeah," he said. "Well, it's a lot more sensitive than the older machines, that's for sure."

Lyle squinted in the afternoon sun. "You really think this is worth what they wanted for it?"

Jeremy paused, and took a breath to keep himself from smiling; Lyle had been farming at least twice as long as Jeremy'd been alive. He hadn't called the store for a demonstration. He'd called because he wanted to talk to somebody about his new toy.

"Lot of guys around here swear by it," said Jeremy. "We had a couple guys order Case four-fifties but those were construction firms, big projects. Pretty popular with the guys that have 'em. Anyway, most everybody loves the joystick once they get used to it."

"Well, I guess I'll get used to it," Lyle said; in the light, his tanned, wrinkled face looked like a bronze sculpture.

On the walk back to the barn where Jeremy'd parked his car Lyle detailed his plans: they seemed overambitious for a man of his age. He was going to clear enough space to have a pond put in and stocked with fish, and then he'd be able to fish without having to stay out overnight or drive home after it got dark. "I'm not supposed to drive at night anymore," he said, tapping his thick lenses.

"Seems like a whole lot of work," Jeremy volunteered.

"Yes," said Lyle. He nodded his head over toward the other side of the highway, still distant but visible from the path they were walking. "But I had a crew come in to build that place a few years ago and they could probably handle it."

Jeremy looked at the house across the highway, all beige vinyl siding and pristine rain gutters: it was hard to feel like it'd ever really look like it belonged, but that was only because he'd seen a little of how things had been around here once upon a time. In truth it was places like Lyle's that weren't going to fit in pretty soon: white paint on wood, tall rusty windmills out front. They looked like movie props, even to some of the locals.

As they walked, they passed an old shed, boards visibly loosening from the frame—it was an antique, the real thing, something whose nails had earned the right to rust. "Don't make 'em like that anymore," Jeremy said: it was more reflex than remark.

Lyle grinned. "Well, now, that's true, but how would you know anything about that?" he said. He was only teasing, the way a grandfather might.

"I've spent a little time in the country here and there," he said, smiling, and he heard the way it sounded: like they were just a couple of guys talking about the things guys talk about when they run out of business to attend to. But his mind was racing privately backward, as through a dark tunnel, to the interior of the Collins shed, sixteen months ago now: the mounted camera, and the silver fuzz of the boom mic, and the built-up lighting rigs with their bright bulbs screwed into old flash housings probably salvaged from the junk heap; Stephanie standing quietly in the corner, bearing witness, declining Sarah Jane's offer to go wait in the car: "It might be easier"; and then the questions, smooth staccato under a slur riding the hairpin to a foreseeably blunt climax, losing their rising intonations as their numbers gathered, one after another, calm at first and then emerging in their true forms, all the shades of hurt and outrage and buzzing currents of hot anger trying to make contact with the ground, Jeremy ready for it, open to it, as if his gently meandering path had been leading him gradually over the years to a night like this: to find himself alone among the nameless vanished in seeing Lisa as she was, wanting to help her even if it meant getting hurt. It rushed in on him quickly, but he had learned young how to consign hard thoughts to hidden corners, and he sent it all back to its permanent home: a space that resembled, in one part, the place where people in the movies said they stored memories of their weekends in Las Vegas, and which resembled, in its greater part, nothing like those weekends at all.

"Well, that's good," said Lyle; at the sound of his voice Jeremy's thoughts scattered like light mist from the surface of water. "There'll be less and less of it to see after a while, I guess."

"I guess that's right," said Jeremy, trying without success to stop his mind's eye from conjuring up an unattended Super Boom, and, failing that, trying not to watch as it plowed directly into an old wooden shed: the teeth of the bucket shiny and sharp, the CPU gone berserk, everything over in less than a minute—the shock of impact, the satisfying crunch of boards cracking under hard steel, the muffled sounds of everything inside being quickly crumpled into unrecognizable pulp.

PART FOUR

✳

1   They were carrying the film equipment down to the cellar: dusty, unwieldy old machines, enlargers and old rollers and cases of emulsion and fixer. There was nowhere else in the house to put it all. This place was going to fill right up as soon as the rest of the moving trucks got here, you could see it. There was about a week left to squirrel away all the stuff they'd asked Abby to send ahead first, and then the flood would come.

Moving didn't seem to strain their marriage the way it did other people's. They had plenty of friends who'd moved once and talked about it like they'd survived wartime: how they'd eaten on the floor for several weeks, how they'd had to buy new towels they didn't even need, how they'd gotten so tired of all the takeout places in their new town that even now, years later, they'd shudder driving past the Long John Silver's.

It wasn't like that at all for Ed and Emily. Credit the late start. They'd stayed put until James and Abby were both old enough to go to college, then told them on Abby's first Christmas back from school—James's third—that they were going to sell the house and move someplace where they could see the seasons change.

Abby cried; her first semester at Reed had been lonely and cold. The last few weeks of waiting to come home were torture.

She'd had to spend Thanksgiving in Portland; her aunt Doris was a widow who lived up on the northeast side, and they'd had chicken cordon bleu at an old card table together in the living room, which was sweet and cozy. But it made going back to the dorm later even worse. Her expanding horizons made it impossible to think about how much she missed West Covina without feeling weirdly provincial, for a Californian, but she was honest with herself about it. She missed the freeways, the clustering strip malls. She missed all of it, and now her parents were taking it away.

They'd been understanding but firm: they were sympathetic, but they had their own dreams now. New Mexico. The Rockies. Wherever the road took them. "It was how we lived when we were young," Ed Pratt said, sizing up both kids, now grown so big. He and Emily had agreed, before setting out on the path of parenthood, that it was important to be honest with your children; they had made good on that promise. For the children, this had always been a mixed blessing.

"Come on, Ab," James said, reaching for another slice of pizza. "You knew they were outta here as soon as they got rid of us." He smiled; he was teasing his father, who cared too much about things.

"They're going to sell the house!" she said.

"We're going to sell it," Emily Pratt said to her daughter, gently but conclusively. "Not right away, but before you graduate, Ab. And then we're going to take half the money with us, and put the other half into an interest-bearing account in your names."

James and Abby exchanged a glance, weighing their losses against the promise of new gains.

"We've had it all planned out for a while, now."

"We're buying an RV," offered Ed.

"Good Lord," said James, but Abby knew then that he was right: they'd been looking forward to this, and it was final.

She picked a few olives off her own slice of pizza with her fingernails, scooting them as far to the side as they'd go without falling off the plate.

"Well, I know you guys will be happy to be out having adventures," she said, visibly trying so hard to be the good grown-up her parents had hoped to raise that her mother burst into tears right there in the middle of Round Table Pizza.

Emily'd picked up the camera equipment at a going-out-of-business sale the following October: Colima Film and Foto had been a neighborhood fixture for years, but nobody could fight the digital tide. Fotomats with their windows boarded over had briefly been a common sight in grocery store parking lots; the ones that didn't convert to cappuccino stands got knocked down and bulldozed so quickly the eye forgot they'd ever been there in no time at all.

It all seemed to happen nearly overnight. She brought in a roll of film she'd shot in Santa Fe during the second semester of James's sophomore year at college, where the grievances he continually aired against St. John's had become almost comically transparent affectations. ("Too many hippies," he said dismissively while looking out his dorm window, but Mom was young enough to recognize the music he'd turned down when she arrived: it was *Meddle*.) "You'll have to pick these up by next Friday," Kurt said: he owned the place and was usually the only person in the store. "Friday's the last day."

She looked around the store, her eyes suddenly registering yellow tags on everything. "What? Why?"

He reached into his pocket and brought out his iPhone, holding it up lens side out. "We're not really needed any more," he said. He was old enough that the suggestion of retirement fit naturally over

165

his general appearance—the patches on his corduroy coat, the thick bifocals. But his choice of words suggested several feelings mixed together, and she wondered what would replace the little store next to the Teleflora.

She picked up a Nikon F from a crowded table in front of the counter: it was in terrific condition, sharp and clean. "Oh, Kurt, for pity's sake," she said when she saw the bright "50% Off!" tag hanging from the rewind knob: a vision of Kurt's garage, swollen with equipment he'd never use or need, had begun rapidly establishing a foothold in her imagination. Dusty tripods and frames were huddled together there in the shadows, conspiring to make her feel sad.

"It's all right," he said. "I'm ready for some kind of new adventure. Hauling all the big stuff in back out to the dumpster's going to be the worst part."

She insisted, over his protests, on paying him ("Seriously, you're doing me a favor," he said); he made sure she allowed him to arrange the transport. It all sat in a pile next to mops and buckets for a month or so, but that first autumn with both kids gone she registered for night classes at Mount San Antonio College and enrolled in two the following spring: Basic Digital and Film Photography, and Laboratory Studies: Black and White. Older students are often the best students. They know they may not have another chance to learn.

By May she'd built a little darkroom in the garage. It was a good way to spend her mornings dabbling, waiting for Ed to come home from work. He had another year to go before he retired from Charter Oak. He was working half days now and they'd cut his caseload in half. He enjoyed these unspooling days; his clients got more of him, because he had more to give. One day there'd be no more clients at all; he'd see his last one, say goodbye to everyone, and then set out for the great unknowable beyond. It wouldn't be long at all.

By the time they got to Iowa they'd been on the road for over a year, Ed at the wheel of the RV he'd christened the *Greener Pastures*. They spent their first summer in Ashland, Oregon, in a bungalow Ed's old classmate George Plummer planned to put on the market in the fall. He, too, was retiring; he'd traipse all over Europe one last time and then move into a condo smack dab in the middle of Portland. "I had a good run here but I still feel kinda cramped," he told Ed, who smiled all night listening to George spin stories about his practice in southern Oregon: he ran a rehab that also had outposts in Medford and Eugene. He was selling those, too. Condos in Portland were fetching enormous prices.

When George got back home in September, he put up the FOR SALE sign ("You have to see Romania before you die," he told them), and they headed east: they hit campgrounds in Montana and North Dakota, but it was the Black Hills in late autumn where they began to first feel vaguely called toward something. It wasn't the adventure that they'd needed after all: it was the light, and the quiet, and the space. Emily's cameras glutted themselves on streams and shadows, but the film had to hibernate in canisters in her backpack.

They found the Collins place listed in an *Advertiser* at a diner the following spring—they were in Missouri, but the real estate listings were from all over the region.

Quaint family farm in quiet location, it said. Farming! The places life takes you if you'll only let it. It took a few months to get all the particulars ironed out, but in the end it felt easy, natural.

When they called, Abby arranged for her parents' things to be sent to them from a U-Stor off the 60 in Diamond Bar; they'd be here soon. But this week there was only the first truck: a table, a bed, the sofa, books and bookcases, and the film equipment from the garage, finally finding its way to a home in a cellar underneath the most darling little farmhouse in central Iowa.

2   The cellar seemed immense, given the modesty of the house above it: without doors and walls and separate rooms to break up the space, it felt like a huge, empty arena. The dirt floor, leveled and smoothed down many years ago, was cool and dry, and the bare-beamed walls were sturdy; with work, it might all have been remade into a proper basement, had Emily not been just delighted with it exactly as it was. "Oh, Ed," she'd said, squeezing his elbow when they first stood at the light switch at the foot of the stairs, seeing the whole of the room at one glance. "It's like some great secret chamber."

It was a big operation, hauling all her equipment down the narrow wooden stairs. Initially she'd reckoned the outbuilding off the driveway as an ideal darkroom: from the outside it looked modest and self-contained, a perfect working space. But inside it was full of equipment, she wasn't sure what for: aluminum tripods and grubby canvas bags, a folding chair and several hundred feet of coiled yellow vinyl-coated polypropylene rope. It'd be shot through with daylight during waking hours, at any rate; its roof sat loosely atop the frame. The cellar was much better.

When all the equipment had been reassembled and rearranged to resemble an easier, more spacious version of the setup she'd fashioned for herself in their West Covina garage, she went back to the shed aboveground: those lights might be useful for something. Her darkroom, curtains and all, only took up one corner of the cellar, the far one, safe from any stray light from the door at the top of the stairs. A lifetime's accumulation of books and keepsakes were in boxes stacked three high against the near wall. The remaining space to the right of the boxes they'd set up as a TV nook; neither Ed nor Emily had any interest in the television, but the kids might, if they visited. They plugged the old Magnavox into a power outlet in the basement's northeast corner, and Ed heaped some old couch cushions in a pile against the wall next to it.

Emily felt vindicated. Back in West Covina he'd tried to convince the movers to haul the whole couch off to the Goodwill, but she'd caught wind of the arrangement in time. "Let's at least keep the cushions," she'd said: they were yellowish green, a little grotesque. For her, they brought back fond and now quite distant memories of her first pregnancy, when the couch, new and modern, had been the most comfortable seat in the house.

When, having rearranged them into a tidy stack, she turned around to view the room again, Ed saw the expression on her face: in the year they'd spent out on the road, they'd grown accustomed to the vagabond life, keeping possessions down to a minimum and making do with materials at hand. But now, all this old stuff, the chairs and the bookshelves and the cushions, were a line out to the time before they'd set off on their adventures: to the long gathering time that had made all their adventuring possible in the first place, over forty years of diligent, almost unconscious preparation.

"You were right, you were right," he said, smiling.

———

It was the first weekend that June when James and Abby arrived; he flew from Albuquerque and she came from Portland, and both their connecting flights articulated in Dallas.

"How long are you gonna stay?" James asked his sister while they waited at the gate. The airport was crowded, busy, and loud, televisions and gate-change announcements competing unsuccessfully for attention over the sporadic beeping of utility shuttles.

"All summer?" said Abby. "I don't know. My dorm doesn't open back up until August. I don't have anywhere else to go."

"How's Reed?"

"Portland is the *best*," she said. "I want to stay after I graduate." James felt a pang of jealousy; he couldn't wait to leave New Mexico behind.

"You've been there a year," said James.

"But there's so *much* going on in Portland," she said. "It's all right there, you just walk everywhere. Or take the bus. You don't have to even have a car. I don't know. I just fell in love with it all sometime during the winter. For two days we had *snow*."

"Maybe you'll fall in love with *Collins*," he said.

She raised her eyebrows and pursed her lips. "Maybe *you* will," she said, ducking out of the way before he could punch her on the shoulder.

"It's just a gigantic dirt lot," said James. Abby'd burst into tears upon seeing her mother in the driveway: parents get so old when you leave them to themselves for a few semesters. But the men lingered outside by the old corncrib. James wanted to see what he was in for, and Ed was eager to see his only son's eyes taking the place in for the first time.

"No, it's a field," said Ed.

"Fields have grass on them."

"Well, there's actually some pretty tall grass to cut through once you get all the way out there to the trees," Ed laughed. "We gave up before we got through it. But whoever was here last tilled under the crop at the end of the harvest, anyway. There's actually some stuff coming up if you go out and look."

James pointed toward the trees. "You guys planning on opening a junkyard?"

People have expectations of a field: what one ought to be like, how it ought to feel. But a field is what you make of it. The dilapidated bus and the gutted Oldsmobile in the tall grass out by the ancient black walnut trees at the far end of the property bequeathed a vague squalor to the otherwise empty field that abutted the Collins house, easy to miss if you scanned the lot quickly but hard to shake off once you'd registered them there, rusty and dry in the early summer sun.

James started out across the field, his father behind him.

I lived in Colo, Iowa, for a couple of years. It's right up the road, really. I was in a holding pattern, waiting to know what to do with myself next. I worked one harvest on a grain elevator; it was punishing work, and everyone seemed a little surprised that I was up to the task. They never said so, of course. There isn't a lot of unnecessary conversation on a grain elevator.

I manned the west site a time or two: it had a grate into which trucks could dump soybeans. It was my job to open the back of the truck and turn on the belt that carried the beans to the bin. There were two, maybe three small silos, as I remember: it's been a long time.

In a small grass lot on the other side of the silos were several abandoned cars. I have always wondered how a thing as big as a car comes to be abandoned: Does somebody drive it to its destination, knowing this will be the end of the line? Does a driver one day say, that's it, this car has broken down on the road one time too many, I can't stand it any more, no one will ever want this car, I'm just going to leave it here? Do junkyards tow cars too stripped to be of value to distant fields and unhook them in the middle of the night?

There was a lot of junk in these cars, which I took the liberty of investigating more closely one cold November afternoon when the trucks were coming in slowly, no more than two or three an hour. There were admissions packets from DMACC and crumpled Marlboro 100 packs. There were clothes—a thin pink cardigan, some sweat socks—which seemed very sad to me. On the seat of one car there was a dildo with a plastic handle at its base; it looked to have been wrested from a display case somewhere.

I didn't ask my coworkers at the grain elevator if they knew anything about whose cars these might have been or why they'd been left there. They would have found the question odd, and probably embarrassing, especially coming from me. Who cares about some junked cars in a grass lot over by the west site? My house, when I lived in Colo, stood directly across the street from the west site; when I finally moved out, in September of 1994, the cars behind the bins were still there. If, in all the years that have passed between then and now, anyone has thought of them, it was probably only to say that they meant to take care of them somehow, someday, and that the parts might be worth something, so they weren't ready for the junkyard just yet.

"Holy shit, the keys are in the ignition," James said when he and his father had reached the rusting body of the Oldsmobile.

Ed smiled, out exploring in the great wide world with James, his once-small companion. Just like old times. "Be pretty surprised if the engine turns over," he said, so pleased to find himself here, now, a grown man talking with his son about this gutted husk of a car. You have to guard moments like these ones, and you do it by keeping them quiet. You never know how many more you're going to get.

"I'm going to open the trunk," said James.

3   The first tape was just street scenes: no commentary, no known locations, no titles. The locales varied—there were park benches, and bus stops, and grassy hills by freeway off-ramps. In all these places two constants remained: people, and garbage. There were men and women in dirty clothes, digging through trash cans, sometimes scrounging in the nearby grass, eating with their hands, casting furtive glances around as they ate; often, when they'd left the scene, the camera would remain trained on the spot, as if waiting for something new to develop. Nothing did. Five minutes would pass with no action in the frame, then seven. There was no news to report after the garbage eaters had gone, but the camera, possibly mounted and left unmanned, kept at its work until someone remembered to turn it off. The scene would end then, cutting out abruptly, and just as suddenly the next scene would begin: static, familiar, identical save for the particulars.

"It's somebody's college project," James offered. The army-green plastic garbage bag full of videotapes from the trunk of the Oldsmobile bulged on the cellar floor nearby.

"No way," said Abby. "This took years."

"Big expert," said James.

She pointed at a teenage girl on the screen. "Those are

acid-washed," she said. "Eighties." She picked up the remote, hit PAUSE for a second, then REWIND. The footage scrolled backwards for a minute, then two.

"There," she said, hitting PLAY again. A woman in jeans, a halter top, and oversized brown sunglasses was stopped mid-stride. "Those are Dittos. Mid-seventies."

"You ever heard of this amazing invention called the thrift store?" said James, more out of habit than conviction.

"There's no way," she said. She froze the screen again and pointed in sequence at several spots. "Macramé purse. Birken-stocks."

She let it play for another minute.

"Orange polyester pants," she said triumphantly.

"Are you spending Mom and Dad's retirement studying fash-ion design?"

"It's weird, at Reed we have these courses in this subject they're tentatively calling 'history.' Deeply experimental."

James watched, again, the woman with the macramé purse, who paused to talk to the people scavenging in the garbage: the camera's station, no nearer than across the street, was too far off to pick up any dialogue. Traffic obscured the view from time to time.

"You're right," he said after a minute. A green car rolled slowly into the frame from the right, accelerating suddenly. "Jesus, that's a Gremlin. Those things are legendary." More cars passed: big Fords like boats, several Honda hatchbacks in quick succession.

"They're all scenes of basically the same stuff happening over a long period of time," Abby said when they'd been sitting in silence for a while.

James didn't know what to say. He was curious. Curiosity had always felt, to him, like something you ought to be ashamed of, an accusing finger pointing out that there's something you don't know yet.

"There's no label on the tape?" he said finally, cross-legged on the floor in front of the television down in the cellar.

"It just says *Street Number Five* on the container," said Abby, sliding the TDK-branded cardboard shell from the top of the VCR and handing it over even though she'd already told him all there was to know about it.

"Half of this is going to be porn," said James; Abby was arranging the tapes into tidy stacks on the floor. Some were missing; all nine of the *Street* series were present and accounted for in all their excruciating tedium, but others, judging from their titles, were from the middle of a sequence. *Driveway 5–7. Church Services 3.*

"You hope," said Abby.

"I hope I get to watch porn with you, Abs?" he said, eyebrows up. "Am I hearing this right? I just want to make sure I understand what it is you imagine I'm thinking."

She emulated the universally recognizable voice of the stupid older brother, laying it on thick: "'I just watched ninety minutes of people at a bus stop. I bet the next tape's porn.'"

James laughed; she was right. "It'd be better than if it's all bus stops," he said.

She tallied her win on a scorecard in her head and let him off the hook. "These nine are *Street*," she said. "There's also *Field*, three of those but they're numbered one, three, and four. Then two with a bunch of two-letter combos in a row but no numbers, *MN IA NE SD* on the one and then *MO IA SD* on the other."

"Minnesota, Iowa, Nebraska, South Dakota."

"Wow, they're really working you hard out there at St. John's," she said.

"We get to write our own majors, I picked State Abbreviations. Very forward-looking place," said James.

"You're really funny now!" she said without insult: he'd always tried, but now he talked like a grown-up instead of a teenager who hopes people laugh at his jokes.

"Thanks," he said, looking around to change the subject. She'd finished stacking the contents of the first box, fifteen tapes: the nine *Streets*, the three *Fields*, the two with the state abbreviations, and one marked *Shed #4*.

"Just the one *Shed*," said Abby, picking it up, turning it over in case there was something else written on it somewhere: some initials in ballpoint, a date. Nothing.

"Maybe the others are in that other box," James suggested.

She fed it to the VCR, whose gears turned loudly as the tape slid in. It worked fine, but it was an old machine.

The action began immediately.

The unedited *Shed #4* is hard to watch. It's long; shot with a Samsung SCF34 onto a Fuji 120 Super VHS Pro tape, it is a single continuous take. From the opening shot of the unoccupied outbuilding, its chair ready to receive, right down to the lingering view of the field at night after the fleeing woman hits the vanishing point, there's no break in the play: everything happens in real time. They bring her in; they attach her to the chair; they begin asking her questions, footage that was never transferred to copies of *Against All Odds* or *Pale Rider* or *Fresh Horses* and so remained unseen until James and Abby retrieved the tape from the trunk of the Oldsmobile. She rises to her feet, as we've seen, standing on one leg as though bidden; and then, as Steve and Jeremy and Shauna can attest, she breaks for the driveway. She's pursued by a two-man skeleton crew: whoever's holding the camera, and Lisa Sample, whose familiar body we see briefly in the frame when the action goes off-script.

"Sorry," says the cameraman, whose name has not been preserved.

"God *damn* it," says Lisa, knocking the camera from his hands.

When the tape ran out the machine began rewinding automatically. The blue screen showed frost-white chunky numbers scrolling backwards, too fast for the eye to follow.

"What the fuck," said James, watching the counter: it was comforting. "What the *fuck*."

"Can you stop saying 'what the fuck'?" said Abby; she was standing over her stacks of tapes, regarding them as a farmer might consider a nest of snakes.

"Go tell Mom and Dad about this," James said.

"Leave Mom and Dad alone."

"It was on their property, they should know about it."

"It's somebody's AV project from the stupid state university," she said. She was angry; it had been impossible to look away from the television the whole time, but she'd come away feeling dirty. The sensation registered in her shoulders and upper arms, an unwelcome burden beginning to establish its weight.

"It's a fucking home movie," James said, snatching up a tape from the as-yet unsorted box: *Interviews #3*. "The worst AV student in the world knows better than to shoot trash like that. There's no titles, no edits, no nothing. There's just—"

The tape finished rewinding and auto-ejected, and James

deftly made the switch; he hit PLAY, and the screen blurred into focus, a young man's face in close-up, head lowered as if in expectation of some reprimand, waiting for something.

"Just *nothing*."

Abby looked at her brother, down there doing his best to put on an air of authority, and then she looked back over to the tapes, adding up the numbers. A hundred and twenty minutes, two hundred and forty minutes, four hundred. Six hours in three tapes, twelve hours in six, twenty-four hours in twelve.

"Years," she said. "It would take years."

The door from the kitchen creaked open and light flooded down the steps. The kids had been in the basement for what seemed like forever.

"Whatcha watchin'?" Emily Pratt asked with a big smile when she got to the bottom of the stairs. It was great to have the kids around after being without them for so long out there on the road. It's hard to describe, this feeling of seeing your kids spending time together like adults, meeting up again after being out there in the world like free agents: there's something giddy and unreal about it. I knew that boy when he was afraid of strangers. I knew them both before they knew how to talk.

4   "I don't see anything," Stephanie says, scrutinizing the city scene before her.

"Just there," Lisa says. "By the garbage."

The woman near the trash bin seems oblivious to the other people at the bus stop. She leans over the hole and plunges her arm in, fishing around down there, her forehead pressing into the rim. She retrieves half of something wrapped in butcher paper, maybe a sandwich or some cheese, and drops it into a tote bag that hangs from her left shoulder. You can see her breath in the air: it's winter somewhere.

"Oh," says Stephanie.

"There's more," says Lisa, holding down the VOLUME button on the remote, the green bars on the screen increasing their numbers in response. City sounds from the speaker on the cabinet: trucks, sirens, horns.

"I want to go home," Stephanie says.

"A lot of people want to go home," says Lisa, her anger like a musket flashing in the dark.

"What are you doing?" demands Jeremy from his chair. Lisa cocks her head to one side, regarding him with what looks like pity or scorn.

"I'm trying to find my mother," she says, locating her inner balance again, the center from which she tries hard not to stray.

"Jeremy Heldt," he says. The light is hot on his face.

"Your full name."

"Jeremy James Heldt."

"Ever 'JJ'?"

"No, just Jeremy."

"Simple Jeremy."

"That's right," he says.

"Why are you here?"

"Like I told you. After I saw the place earlier—"

"You were here earlier."

"Well, you know I was, you were here too."

"Please tell the camera that you came here earlier today."

If you rented one of the two copies of *A Civil Action* that stood, for several years, on the shelves of Movies & More in Tama, you may already have seen and heard Jeremy's response. It was edited into one of the scenes toward the end of the movie, after the class action suit gets dismissed. Unlike Lisa's earlier work, this edit feels natural; there's no way to make real sense of it in the context of the movie, but you might imagine some mix-up further up the line—something gone wrong in mastering, maybe, a documentary scene cut in by accident. Removed from the greater context of the interview within which they were made, Jeremy's remarks seem cryptic, and it's hard to account for the severity of his tone.

"I was here earlier today," he says. There's a silence, and a possible edit. "I came out here earlier to say I'm starting a new job and it's full-time. On the way here I saw Ezra in the road and I pulled over. I didn't know he was coming out here. I helped clean up the road and I drank a glass of water and then I went home, and I called Stephanie after I woke up because when I saw the driveway of your house, I recognized it."

Lisa's voice, offscreen, sounds suddenly warm now; it's hard to account for it. "How did you recognize my driveway?" she says.

"From the movies," says Jeremy.

"I'm calling the cops right now," Stephanie said in the car. Out on these country highways late at night the stars ripple like great sparkling banners overhead. Jeremy headed steadily for the brighter lights: Ames in the distance.

He reached over from the driver's seat, putting his hand over Stephanie's cell phone. "Don't," he said.

"I am calling the police!" she said. "You can't be OK with this!"

"We're not hurt," he said. "Don't."

"You are so weird!" She was yelling, frustrated by how he kept his eye on the road while he argued. "You've always been weird! You're sick like her!"

"I'm not sick. We're not hurt," he said again. "There's something wrong with her. She can't help it. Don't."

Stephanie stared at Jeremy, trying to understand his apparent calm. It would be morning soon. They'd been kept there all night. How could he stand it?

"How can you stand it!" she said.

"Put yourself in her shoes," Jeremy said evenly, and it felt like a knife pushing through his chest from the inside, because he knew Stephanie would not be able to understand—Stephanie, whose mother and father lived together in a house less than a mile from the apartment she rented, whose parents would grow old together and someday be buried next to each other in a plot in the Nevada

City Cemetery, their children and grandchildren gathering to honor two lives well lived.

"Try to put yourself in her shoes," he repeated when she gave no response, leaving it out there in the opening silence, the spring night air.

Lisa in mid-frame; a voice offscreen: Sarah Jane Shepherd, sounding steady and confident, sure of her purpose. She has never considered herself a religious person, but this morning—as they prepare, on short notice, to leave the house in Collins, each to their own errands: Sarah Jane back to Nevada, Lisa to parts unknown—she feels a vague sense of kinship with former coworkers from back when she worked retail; people who used to tell her, on their lunch breaks together around a tiny table in a supply room, that God had a plan for everybody.

"Are you ready?" she says.

"I think so," says Lisa.

"Whenever you're ready," says Sarah Jane.

"It helps if you ask questions."

"OK." There's a beat; birds chirping nearby somewhere, greeting the day. "Where did you grow up?"

"A couple of places."

"Where were you born?"

"Down in Tama." Lisa smiles. "You already know all this stuff."

"OK." A silence. Lisa looks at the lens, waiting. "OK, then. Why do you make these movies?"

Over the years, she has taken great pains to hide the face of the child she once was. She does it by trying to feel older than she is. She began this practice when she was young; it made her feel better the first time she tried, so she kept at it. Over time it has been

184

a great comfort, this discipline of imagining herself alive and intact, safe on the other side of years she might otherwise have had to live through, uncertain of where they would lead. The camera catches her out now; there's a part of her that never left Crescent, that still waits there for someone.

"For my mom," she says.

"How do you mean, for your mother," asks Sarah Jane.

"I wanted her to be able to tell her story," says Lisa slowly.

"But we don't even know what her story is."

"Well, to do her a kindness, I guess."

"But she can't really receive that kindness."

"It's so she won't be forgotten," says Lisa, looking pleadingly into the lens.

"But there's nothing you can do about that," Sarah Jane presses. "And besides, Lisa—I don't really see how any of this helps with any of that. They don't seem connected. You have to see that."

"Look, I do it for myself, too, I know that," says Lisa, casting her gaze out now past the tripod, around it and out to the tall rows of corn on the neighboring property, the pigs in the distance. "I don't see why you have to make me say it out loud."

She gets up then, walking past the mounted camera, and there's an extended quiet during which we can't see that she's gone to stand beside the friend she made of the lonely woman from Nevada; the two of them looking out from the porch to the corn, and the brace of sycamores farther down, the wind at play in the leaves.

Emily called Ed down to the basement when her gut told her it was time; after they'd all spent a couple of hours watching movies together, they congregated in the living room. This was an unfamiliar scenario for all of them. The Pratts hadn't ever been the sort of family to hold meetings, to regiment their lives like a business. Still, they all took their places on the couches and cushions, like they'd been doing it all their lives.

Ed spoke first, from his heart: "I don't really know what to say." He looked at his children. "Are you both all right?"

By now James had managed to summon up his defenses. "No, Dad, I'm hurt. I watched a lot of *movies*," he said.

"I'd appreciate it if you could be serious," Abby said.

"Thanks, Abby," said Ed. "I mean it, James. We live in a world now where people see things all the time, all kinds of things, and they think nothing ever leaves a mark on them, but—"

"I'm *fine*," said James.

Ed looked at his son, who had fixed his eyes on the floor between his feet. "All right," he said gently. "Just checking in."

He looked over at Emily, whose face was sad.

"I wish we hadn't watched it down in the darkroom," she said. It was her special place in the world. "It will feel different for a while. But I'm all right. I'm not the one who's hurt."

"I'm real glad you guys all feel great," Abby said, exasperated. "Can we talk about those poor *people* now?"

"We'll rescue them, right, Abs?" said James. His recovery was progressing rapidly. "We'll just head out to the driveway, maybe follow their scent out into the cornfields."

"You shut up," said his sister. "That stuff was fucked up. She hit that boy hard enough to leave a bruise on his face. You could see his cheek turning red." Her voice caught in her throat when she described it; she hadn't been able to look away.

Ed felt so proud of his daughter; someday she'd stop seeking the high ground all the time, and she'd be happier for it, but it would mean that the child he'd known so long ago was finally gone forever. It gave him such joy to see her putting that moment off for as long as she could.

"Easy, Ab," he said. She nodded. "There's nothing we can do right now. Let's eat something, and maybe try not to think too hard about it just now, and then we'll think a little more about it tomorrow morning."

The children slept hard; it had been a very long day. The Pratts had some decaf in the kitchen, and then they, too, turned in for the night. Those shaky visions from the basement weren't strong enough to crowd out the pleasure of having everybody under the same roof for the first time in well over a year. Was it two years? Retirement time was a new and disorienting rhythm.

"It's great to see the kids, anyway," Emily said, nuzzling Ed's shoulder in the dark.

"I miss them," said Ed, whispering as if to guard a secret from temperatures in which it wouldn't survive, from the threat of all that open air.

5 James was at the tiny drop-leaf table in the kitchen the next morning—"You have a *breakfast nook!*" Abby'd squealed when she spotted it yesterday, her mother trying not to beam with satisfaction—scowling at his open laptop, muttering incredulously to himself as he scrutinized the upper right corner of the screen. "You have to be kidding," he was saying just as his mother came in.

"You be nice to your parents," she said. "There's Internet on the computer upstairs."

He blinked at her. "Mom, you are the last people in the country who have to plug into the wall to get online."

"Your parents are older than you are," she said, lifting her eyebrows pointedly. "You are the last son in the country to come to this conclusion. We're even."

He rose from his chair, pulled his phone from his pocket, and held it up, screen side out. "Half a bar!" he said. "I can't do *any*thing on half a bar! The *Vatican* is more wired than this place!"

She laughed. "We'll have a wireless router installed when we can, dear," she said. But James, pacing past the kitchen door, had seen his signal suddenly jump, and was hurriedly typing search terms into Safari. *There is nothing wrong with the upstairs computer,* Emily was thinking defensively as her son's attention disappeared into the palm-sized glow. The upstairs computer was a Gateway. It had come in a big box with adorable cow spots on the sides.

"He's twenty minutes away," said James, quietly but excitedly, not looking up, his grip tightening around the phone in his hand. Emily leaned over her son and looked down; a blue dot throbbed atop a highway map. "He's literally twenty minutes away."

"Who is?" said Emily.

"Jeremy Heldt," he said, in a low tone like a Hollywood priest lapsing into church Latin.

I wonder what you see in your mind's eye when I ask you to remember the house in Nevada where Jeremy Heldt used to live. Wood? Brick? Vinyl siding? High windows? A fireplace? Try to remember whether Steve Heldt had a garage to park his car in: Did he? How many cars did it have room for? What kind of cars? Was there a door leading into the house from the garage, as at the Sample house in Crescent, or did the outbuilding stand free, with a little grassy alley between its outer wall and the house's west-facing side? Did the street out front have a sidewalk, or was it one of those more recent developments, a neighborhood planned to keep the riff-raff out: no public thoroughfare, streetlights kept on all night, awkward traffic islands at the four-way stops? If you're able to imagine Steve Heldt grown older now, answering the door, do you hear an accent—something homey, something quasi-Southern?

No. There is no identifiable accent here unless you've cultivated a very careful ear. This is an easy place to live, milder in feel than Nebraska to the west, negligibly warmer in the winter than Minnesota to the north, of less imagined consequence to the world than Illinois to the east or Missouri to the south. The reason you have a hard time seeing the house is that it was built not to stand out. It went up in 1951, and is brick with small four-square windows made of Pella glass, and there is no garage, because most people back then had only one car, and they parked it in the driveway.

"What can I do for you?" said Steve to the young man now standing on his doorstep, a boy who reminded him of his son in scruffier days, in times gone by; maybe all young men remind aging fathers of how their sons once were, years ago.

"I was looking for Jeremy," James said, trying to sound natural.

Steve cocked his head and considered his visitor: the shaggy hair, the flash of silver in the left earlobe underneath the curling locks; the too-smart gray summer blazer, linen or seersucker, stuff nobody wears around here. "Probably have to wait until Thanksgiving," he offered after a moment, smiling. "Who should I say stopped by?"

"Is he all right?" James asked, bluntly, the way people talk where he grew up, and that was when the temperature of the air on the front porch seemed to drop, the two considering each other, spanning a gulf neither could accurately describe.

I wish I could have been there to see it: moments like this were like oxygen for me once. But I had to move on. There's no going back. I lost all my equipment in the move.

Steve Heldt's face froze. "As far as I know," he says, and then: "What's this about? I hope there's nothing wrong," gesturing to the unknown visitor with his free hand and holding the front door open with the other, come in, come in, *tell me nothing's wrong* tolling steadily in the privacy of his heart, the younger man fishing now inside the inner pocket of his coat, retrieving from it a thick eight-and-a-half-by-eleven sheet folded lengthwise, printer stock his mother has on hand for when she plays around with her digital camera in Collins: this printed page bearing the image of a young

190

man in a chair, eyes avoiding the lens, colors badly corrected and gaudy but visibly Jeremy Heldt, young Jeremy as he'd appeared to his friends and family and coworkers over a decade ago.

James took the Lincoln Highway west from Nevada instead of heading directly back to his parents' place. He wanted to clear his head, and he felt starved for time to himself. Back at St. John's, he'd been sharing a dorm room with a computer science major; it was a zero-pressure environment. The discord of finding himself alone in a house with his whole family inside it had been a shock he'd struggled to conceal. Up near the mountains in New Mexico, he sometimes yearned either for their company or for the promise of it, but Collins, however novel, made for close quarters.

Entering Ames, he didn't feel much of a difference—there was a big city park with a wide stream running through it on one side of the highway, and a few auto shops dotting the other—but then the buildings began to form clusters. It wasn't Albuquerque, the place he and his friends liked to spend weekends they later wouldn't remember, but it had an excitement to it all the same. Ames! Who knew anything about Ames, Iowa? But here it was: florists and fast food and four-way intersections where it'd actually make a difference if you ran the red light.

The little downtown was trying to shed some of its quaintness; there was a big abstract steel sculpture on one corner, but across the street stood a statue of an anthropomorphic bird, its cartoon-gloved index finger pointing at the sky: *We're Number One.* The surface of the statue was composed of rectangular shards of reflective glass; its glint was blinding. Down in Las Cruces, New Mexico State had a mascot, a mustachioed cowboy pointing a revolver at an unseen aggressor. You saw him everywhere. His name was Pistol Pete, and his aspect was unambiguous. The mirror-shard bird was harder to read.

But the window of the health food store made him homesick for Santa Fe specifically. He could see the blue corn chips and the expensive bottled water from the street. He was a senior now; maybe he'd take a six-pack back to the farmhouse. Have a beer with Dad. Why not?

Inside Wheatsfield Grocery he felt less uprooted than he'd felt since landing in Des Moines. This could have been anywhere: the same Odwalla juices, the same Kettle chips. A hot bar with sautéed kale and grilled pineapple chicken. The guy with the beard at the checkout had a huge scar running from his elbow to his wrist instead of the tattoos he might have had in Santa Fe, but he was still a guy with a beard.

He was quiet, though; he didn't look up from the scanner while his hands worked, and he didn't return James's attempt at making eye contact. When he scanned the beer, he did say "See some ID?"

James offered his student card from St. John's; the guy with the name tag reading EZRA squinted at it, handed it back, and said: "Need a driver's license for beer."

James still had his California license; he fished it out. "Sorry," he said. Ezra's quiet had the effect of making James want his approval.

"No, it's fine," Ezra said, bagging the groceries. "Lot of students here."

"You go to ISU?" James said.

"No," Ezra said, gently laughing, and then he finally looked up; James felt an intense relief. "I'm just a farmer's kid."

It was a remark with a soft finality to it: I'm just a farmer's kid. You're buying groceries from me at a cooperatively owned and operated store in a university town, but I'm just a farmer's kid. If someone in West Covina at a Sprouts had said this to James, he would have come back with something really smart and cutting, but there was no guile in Ezra's voice. Fluorescent light caught the scar on his arm: the suture marks gleamed. They had to be a few years old.

"Well, thanks," James said. Some people acclimate faster than you think they will. It's not the easiest rhythm in the world to catch, but its ability to roll wordlessly over the depths has a real appeal.

"He's fine, they're all fine," James said from the worm-worn desk in front of the upstairs computer; Mom had bought it for twelve dollars at the monthly auction in Colo, where she'd also bought the antique office swivel chair he was sitting in (five dollars; the seat, back, and arms were solid oak, and the springs creaked loudly) and the lamp he was working by (three dollars, with a porcelain base bearing the image in relief of a bending willow, from Taiwan circa 1970).

"How can they be fine?" Abby said. "Did he specifically say everybody was fine?"

"It was his dad," said James. There was a pop-up window open on the monitor in front of him; the cursor blinked awkwardly, anciently. "His dad said he's fine, he lives in Des Moines now."

"Did you ask him about the videos?"

James swiveled; the chair groaned. "I showed him the print-out," he said. "He got scared something had happened and I told him, no, this was on some movie we found in Collins. He asked me inside and I had a beer with him."

"You did not."

"It was a Milwaukee's Best," said Jeremy with great satisfaction. "'Want a Beast?' the guy said when he grabbed it from the fridge. Just like that: 'Want a Beast?' It was *perfect*."

Abby felt a small, guilty pang of grief for the lurid tableaus she'd drawn up in her head: blood and death, a body buried in the field outside the house. She'd felt so sad for the boy on the tapes, the young man answering questions about his life and his family—specifically about his mother: that long sequence about how she died, and whether she'd lived long after the crash or been killed on impact, and what he and his father had done to make their lives bearable after she'd gone—and then being struck so hard in the face, once, then again, and then a third time, hardest of all, for no immediate reason Ed or Emily or Abby or James could imagine, no matter how many times they replayed the sequence that immediately preceded the attack:—*Do you miss her?*—*Sometimes. Not all the time. At Christmas.*

"Did you tell him what you saw?"

"Abs, no," said James. "You gotta see this guy. He's not old like Mom and Dad, but he's at least in his fifties. When he saw the printout I could tell he thought I was going to tell him his son was dead or something, it was horrible. I told him we found some tapes where a lady was talking to his son, asking him questions, and he goes, oh, yeah, Jeremy used to work at a video store, it was a long time ago. He looked sad."

Abby waited for something else, but James held his hands up on both sides, elbows bent, palms up.

"I just felt like if his son's OK now he doesn't need to hear that a long time ago some bad shit happened to him that he maybe doesn't know about, you know?" he said. "So I go, yeah, we found these movies that used to belong to him, I guess, we thought he might want to have them back, and then he went to a corkboard in his kitchen and copied out his son's e-mail address, which is why I'm up here."

She looked at the screen: Gmail was doing its best to auto-save over the slow connection available to it. James had typed, "Dear Jeremy Heldt," but that was all.

"What do you even say," said Abby.

"I know," said James. "And I was in there, for, like, an hour. It felt pretty empty. There's pictures of the whole family on the walls in the living room but it definitely feels like the only guy who lives there now is the dad."

"What do you talk about for an hour with some guy you don't know alone in his house?"

"I *know*," said James again. "Mainly his son, though. How good his son is at his job."

"That's weird."

"It's not weird, is the thing," said James. "I mean I know it sounds weird, but it didn't feel weird. We just sat there and had a Beast, right, and then he started to cheer up, talking about how his son Jeremy kicks ass at his job, how he got this job back when things looked kind of sketchy but it all turned out great and now they don't even think about how sketchy it was for a little while, because now it's all just great, you know? And my eyes kept drifting over to that picture of their whole family up there, and I thought, I'm not gonna push this guy, everything needs to be just great for him."

Abby thought about going back down into the basement for more tapes, to see who else might have been compelled to identify themselves by name; and about then locating those people, trying to ask them what they remembered about something strange they'd done or been asked to do ten or more years ago; and about where they might go from there, what other roads might lie open. She remembered her own mother's face by the screenlight, that look of worry; Mom loved everyone's children, her heart was like the sun.

"I don't want to abandon all those *people*," she said after a moment's consideration.

"Abs," James said gently. "I've been thinking about this all day. I went out and met the guy's father. Don't take this the wrong way, OK?"

Abby scowled and folded her arms; James was a very arrogant brother sometimes.

"Those people don't even know you exist," he said, and though she felt like she ought to have been offended, she knew he was right.

6   You don't see a lot of grain silos in New Mexico. They're there, of course; silos are the great hidden constant of the industrialized world. But you only ever notice them if you happen to reach the saturation point: if you live across the street from one, say, or if, on your way to work each day, you drive past so many outcroppings of them that you lose count. In the West or down South, you have to go off the main highways to see them. Out here you're bound to see a few.

James remained in the upstairs room after Abby had gone; the glare of the old monitor made his eyes burn, so he scooted the rolling chair over to the window to rest for a minute. He looked out: near the boundary line, diagonally opposite the abandoned cars, stood the remains of an animal enclosure, pigs probably. Its rough wooden beams sagged but held their intended shape; you could picture the whole of it thriving with life some spring morning, spry and noisy, bright and needful. Just over its distal beams, right before the fallow Pratt field gave way to the neatly tilled furrows of the neighboring property, was a pile of discarded wood with bits of rusting wire jutting out from it: something roughly dismantled either by hand or by hatchet, left to warp and splinter in the sun and rain.

To one side of this modest ruin, just before where the grass grew high and wild, was a squat silo, dull silver, with a cap like an inverted funnel. There couldn't be anything in it, could there? James sat and thought. If this house had been empty for some time before Mom and Dad arrived, then any grain left in the silo would be rotten by now, perhaps wholly decomposed. He imagined fermented slurry seeping out into the soil, the ground gradually absorbing it over the course of several frozen winters and thawing springs, no trace left of the process.

At first he didn't like the idea, but as he sat staring through the window, he grew fonder of it: a small place, unmarkably emptied of something that had been there once but found its own way out, mindlessly, without intention, by allowing time and air and its own internal moisture to do the work. A relic of no demonstrable presence. He wondered.

By the time he reached the silo on foot, about ten minutes later—getting there was slower going than he'd envisioned; grass was thick on the ground, and the dirt from which it grew was lumpy and uneven, not the gentle rumpled blanket it appeared to be from the upstairs window—he had a clear picture in his mind of what he'd see there, and it wasn't far off from what he actually found: an empty space enclosed by corrugated tin.

He'd expected a concrete foundation, someplace for grain to safely rest; but the silo stood atop bare earth, stray weeds growing inside it now: pale grasses availing themselves of the small daily ration of sunlight that came through a warping space where some screws had come loose. He could imagine himself staking a claim to someplace like this: finding it as a young boy and designating it a clubhouse or a fort.

But as a young boy, he had been happy; he'd gone to a big school, found many friends and some enemies there, lived a life so busy with errands and activities that there'd been a calendar on his wall by the time he was seven, so he wouldn't lose track of soccer practice and swimming lessons. When he pictured a boy who might make this tiny silo his playhouse, he saw someone whose nearest friend was clear across the neighboring field. It was a lonely thing to imagine.

As his mind idled in the three-quarter dark it also wandered to the contents of the tapes in the second box: the one Abby hadn't gotten around to emptying and arranging on the cellar floor. Were there tapes in it marked *Silo #1*, or *Night Silo*, or *North Boundary*? What was on them? New people, further detail? Of course there is not enough light inside the silo to record anything that happens there beyond the audio, but James wasn't thinking that far ahead. He pictured faces, action; revelations instead of only the solitary sound of our voices in the dark.

The trip back to the house felt shorter than the walk out had been. He went back up to where the computer was. The questions he wanted to answer and the ones he meant to leave alone had coalesced into two distinct groups. Even on his mom's antique connection he thought he could get it all settled by evening.

The old computer tower buzzed and whirred as James fed his scant supply of useful search terms into the browser: the address of his parents' new house; the names by which people had either identified themselves or one another on the tapes; a few names and dates he'd harvested from a property deed among Dad's business papers in the filing cabinet. Current owner, prior residence, date of birth: it was enough.

"Oh, seriously?" he said when he saw a Tripod page as the top result. It was like looking through a telescope into a lost age. "People still use Tripod?"

The page was headlined *THEY WERE OUR SONS AND DAUGHTERS*, and was a place people had gone, in desperation, to put their grief. It boasted all the trappings of the initial expansion of the Internet from college campuses and computer laboratories to the wider world: site design from a template supplied by the host, clip art, and several uncorrected spelling errors in the single paragraph atop the frame. *The Michael Christopher Gathering Also Known As Michael's Friends Has Brainwashed Our Childrern And Our Families. This Is Our Story*, it began, and continued:

> Most of Us Have Spent Many Years Seraching For Those We Have Lost. Now We Can Use the World Wide Web to Share Our Story. Please Use These Pages To Learn About Who Michael Christopher Is And Ask In Your Heart If You Can Help.

James read the text dutifully, but his eyes were drawn irresistibly to the faces underneath it, arranged like portraits in a high school yearbook. He felt the nausea he'd fought back in the basement two days ago return: all this trauma felt private, raw, something to be protected from outsiders. He disliked feeling like a voyeur.

> If You Have Seen Any of the People On This Page, Please Sign Our Guestbook. You Can Also Reach Us By Email. Every Little Bit Helps, We Can Be Reached At MChristopherFamilies@hotmail.com.

He had to click through seven faces and read their stories—of children or parents gone missing, notes left behind, whole lifetimes coming to consist only of loose ends—before he got to Irene Sample.

This is my wife, Irene, the mother of our only daughter, Lisa. Lisa is thirty now. She was Five when Irene was taken from us. Although we are apart now I know we both still miss her every day. I am an old man now but there will always be a place in my home for you, Irene. Lisa lives in Nevada now. She has an apartment there. She would love to See you.

Her hair was in a modest bun; her smile was gentle, unforced. The picture was in black and white and had been taken at a photo studio in a Montgomery Ward. It had so little in common with the world in which James lived most of his life that looking at it made him feel dizzy.

Their grief wasn't his to bear, he knew. But it was inside him all the same, like a secret entrusted to a messenger. He dimmed the monitor to black and closed his eyes; the residual gleam ebbed against his eyelids for the better part of a minute. He felt very tired. He did not return to the site to read the guestbook again, where Jeremy Heldt—in a note read eight times in total, according to a helpful counter at the bottom right corner of the post—shared his small part of the story with no one in particular.

Just wanted to stop by here to say I am sorry for all you have had to go through. I know what it is like to lose your mother. Hope someday you can get the answers you need.

Abby came in; James opened his eyes. "Did you write to him yet?" she said.

"I'm getting to it," he said, reaching for the dial quaintly housed in the right underside of the monitor.

———

They ate dinner all together that night; Emily made a big pasta bake and heated up some dinner rolls. To the parents, this gathering felt miraculous: it was fifteen hundred miles from Collins to West Covina; they hadn't reckoned the other distances collapsed at the table, from Portland and Santa Fe, from the outside silo to the upstairs room. The weird shock of the videotapes James had recovered from the Oldsmobile loaned a sense of common purpose to their reunion now, something easier to approach than the things they'd all been both thinking of and trying not to think about just yesterday morning: advancing age, graduation, their various places in the world.

"So tell me about Nevada," Ed said to his son. He intoned the long initial *a* in Nevada with relish: it takes outsiders forever to get over it.

"I met the dude's dad," said James. "Steve. He says his son is fine and lives in Des Moines and he used to work at a video store."

"And?"

"That's pretty much it," said James, looking around the table. "Abby thinks we should just drop it from there."

"Do you think that?" Ed asked, turning.

"Kind of," said Abby. "I don't know."

"Well," Ed said, and his children both steeled themselves: Dad was about to try to shepherd them toward a conclusion. The opening gambit of Dad's conclusion schtick was always a barrage of questions. "What if these had been just somebody's regular home movies?"

"Dad, I know where you're going with this, but please with the what-ifs," said James. Ed looked back at him with wonder, trying to suppress his delight: he didn't want to condescend; there's a complex but palpable joy in seeing your children outgrow you. "There are three things we can do, OK? One, we can watch all the tapes

202

and keep finding people if they say their names and check up on them. No, right?"

He waited, looking around the table, then continued. "Two, we go to the horse's mouth and talk to the guy whose name we do know, which we can do because his father gave me his e-mail address. Jeremy." Ed and Emily exchanged a glance; none of this was news to Abby, but she followed along, enjoying the mildly ridiculous but still impressive persona James had adopted, its ad hoc expertise cut just today from whole cloth.

"Or we don't do anything," said Emily, certain she'd arrived at James's third possibility. "We talk more about why this bothers us and respect that it's not our affair."

"No, Mom," said James. "I mean, yes, to me that's obvious, but Abby hates that one."

"Would you just tell them?" Abby said.

"She made me send the e-mail," he said. Everybody exhaled quietly.

"We decided together," protested Abby.

"That's what you've been doing up there all afternoon?" said Emily.

"I looked at a few other things first. Abby was right, it was all a dead end."

"Has he written back?" Ed asked, visibly concerned.

"It took him, like, a minute," James said, measuring his tone; he felt his father's need for something close to a definitive *yes*, something to shift the conversation back into the world of known quantities. "He sent me the address of the woman asking him questions on the tape. She lives in Tama. It's less than an hour from here."

He was holding something back; families can tell. They waited.

"He also said to leave her alone," James said, finally. " 'You should leave her alone,' is exactly what he wrote. 'You probably won't. I know how it is. I've seen it personally. But I wish you would.'"

They looked around, and down at their plates.

"He's right," said Abby resolutely.

"I know he's right," said James.

"Is it going to make a difference?" asked Abby.

"No," said James.

"Was there anything else?" said Ed.

"He said never to write to him again. Not in a mean way, I don't think," said James. "'I know you probably have a lot of questions, but I would appreciate it if you would please not write to me again. Don't take this personally but all this stuff is none of your business. Sincerely, Jeremy Heldt.'"

"'Sincerely'?" said Abby.

"'Sincerely,'" James repeated, and Emily Pratt, alone among his audience, caught the sadness in his voice, this mood of concern for a stranger whose need to insulate himself from some unknown grief seemed both so clear and so hard to claim. It made her feel proud, to have a son like James.

When the pasta was all gone they finished off the dinner rolls. Any casual onlooker would have thought they were locals.

7   In most lives, in most places, people go missing. This isn't as true as it was in a less connected age; people see more of their high school classmates on Facebook every day than they previously would have in their entire lives after graduation. Lonely husbands or wives form secondary accounts to keep track of lost loves and secret prospects; short of catastrophe, these points of contact never wholly erode. They may go ignored for months or years, but they crackle away in the cables, never wholly out of reach.

In Iowa we had a head start on this whole process, because when we gather on the Fourth of July or at Christmas, we find joy in tracing movements. The habit travels with us; whether we end up moving to Worthington or Owatonna or to the Black Hills in South Dakota, we maintain keen interest in what became of whom, whether we knew them well or not. If somebody in upper management at Mahindra got to talking with Mike about smallmouth bass at the annual expo in Des Moines and ended up offering him a package with better benefits, then that was how Mike and his family ended up in Troy: we may never see Troy with our own eyes, but we'll know where Mike and the kids are all the same. Bill went back to Ashton. Oh, is that right? Yes, he never warmed up to Storm Lake, he feels more at home when he's near where the folks used to live. Yes, that's what Davy said, too; well, but he goes by Dave now, I think he only ever spent two years outside of Urbandale in his life. From Ashton to Bangkok to Spirit Lake to Ventura, and onward, to points further west beyond the imagination, we keep track of our own. It would feel like putting on airs to call it our passion, but it's hard to know what else to call it. It's sufficient work until it comes time to part ways, which we always must do, too soon sometimes.

Did anybody ever hear from Stephanie? Yes, she's teaching again; she was in Ames for a while at Fellows Elementary, they say she had a gift with the special needs kids, but she's not there any more, I don't think, when I saw her at the Wheatsfield Grocery she said she still missed Chicago. Just recently? No, it was a while back, Ezra was working the counter, he looks so different from when he was young and still limps a little from the accident. Do his parents still farm? Yes, his father will still be hauling beans to the Farmer's Exchange in that antique tractor with the cart behind it until he's ninety-three, it's all he knows how to do. But didn't Ezra go off to school in Nebraska? Well, sure, but how's he going to just turn around and be a Big Red guy for the rest of his life, everybody knew he'd be back. You know that nice secretary friend of Steve Heldt's was a Cornhusker, though. She came to visit in the hospital. But Steve never remarried, did he? No, it didn't work out, I guess. He says they still get dinner sometimes, though. I think it's nice.

It's not that nobody ever gets away: that's not true. It's that you carry it with you. It doesn't matter that the days roll on like hills too low to give names to; they might be of use later, so you keep them. You replay them to keep their memory alive. It feels worthwhile because it is.

———

What will you do now? Lisa asks Sarah Jane, off camera.

I guess I'll just go back home, Sarah Jane replies.

You were putting the house up for sale, says Lisa.

No serious buyers, says Sarah Jane. The agent says it could take months.

Lisa's throat convulses when she tries to stifle her sobs. Sarah Jane's face, in the frame, shows compassion, empathy, and hurt. Her time with Lisa will seem like a strange dream of middle age in later years: some people take their savings and travel to Europe when they feel restless, but it costs so much to travel, certainly more than the monthly income from a single video rental store.

It'll be all right, she says. We'll both be all right. She reaches out with her right hand, but Lisa does not reach out to take it.

Lisa's voice is desperate, lost.

Thank you for trying to help, she says.

Of *course*, says Sarah Jane, rising, walking with her arms open toward the tripod and then past it. If you look close you can see from the gentleness of her stride that she would have made a good mother.

The copy of *Burnt Offerings* onto which this scene was transferred is at the Goodwill in Ames next to the Hy-Vee on Lincoln Way. It was left there in the late summer of 2002. It sits on a shelf now next to several dozen other movies like it, back near the books; it's an early VHS, housed in an oversized black plastic shell that's grown old and is cracking along the edge. No one is ever going to take it home and watch it. It will probably be there forever.

There was no RV park in Tama; the nearest one was Shady Oaks, in Marshalltown, and people who parked there had no need to venture further than a highway stop for supplies. So Lisa was surprised to see the *Greener Pastures* coming, advancing steadily down the street. She stood at her window on the second floor and she watched; she couldn't make out the faces of the people inside, but she could imagine them, how they probably looked. The vehicle itself, in the slow pace of the straight line it followed and the cheery tan and yellow of its camper shell, appeared like a seeker after something, certain of its quest but unsure of the path.

Inside the cab they were still arguing. "What exactly are you going to say?" Abby asked for the third time since leaving Collins.

"I'll figure it out," said James. "I figured out Jeremy Heldt."

"I don't know what you figured out," Abby said. "He told you to leave him alone."

"He knew where she was," James said, and though his timing was in their usual fraternal block-and-parry mode, his tone was soft, nurturing. He was guarding something, Abby wasn't sure what. "That's the giveaway."

"He told you not to come here," she said.

"And then he copied and pasted the address from someplace on his hard drive right into the e-mail."

"It's right up there," Ed said from behind the wheel, pointing. They all looked at the house: it was in a nice neighborhood, full of houses that had been built long ago, more ornately decorated than the farmsteads outside Collins or the red-brick duplexes that lined the new streets of Nevada. This one was yellow with brown trim.

"I wouldn't trade the farmhouse for this," Abby said. "I don't know what's wrong with people." She looked through the passenger's-side window of her father's RV with her brow knitted, scrutinizing the little yellow house like something excavated from an archaeological dig. I wished I could have made it last forever: the great hulking machine drawing up to the curb, parking so slowly, not wanting to scrape up the hubcaps, aligning itself and then correcting the angle and finally coming to a stop; the young woman looking out the window, fixing her gaze; and then the whole family, spilling out into the daylight like moles from a hill blasted open, blinking in the bright sun, looking expectantly toward my front porch and then upward to where I stood, happy to have company, smiling and waving like a little girl.

From the window, I couldn't hear what they were saying, of course, but I could see their lips moving. As a child I developed a habit of watching people's mouths when they spoke. In restaurants, for example, with too much ambient noise to make out the words without some visual cue, my father busy with the menu, keeping his idle inventory of which towns called them *hotcakes* and which ones held firm at *pancakes*; but my eye would be on the old woman with her grown-up son two tables away, her eyebrows rising a little as she tried not to telegraph her worry. *You should get a vacation*, she was saying, I was sure of it. You can't miss a word like *vacation*.

Our lives, of course, were in some ways like a vacation that never ended; Dad would find work at the local bank and diligently put in his forty hours, but as soon as he picked me up from school we'd be off on our expeditions: to the shelters, to the hospitals, to the college campuses and the storefront churches. When the options were all exhausted we'd just move on; there are banks everywhere, and if the bank didn't need another accountant, the grain elevator might, or the hog lot, or the fish hatchery.

Wisconsin was where we stopped heading east: we'd spent time in Missouri, and in Kansas, and in Colorado and South Dakota. From there we'd tried Minnesota; Dad had word that the group was active around St. Paul. But Mom wasn't in St. Paul, and she wasn't in Rochester, and while Madison had looked promising— so many Jesus people on the college campuses back then, their feet bare in spring, long hair down to the middle of their backs—the trail had grown cold.

We stayed several years. I was young, but I'd already lived in so many places. Even as a very young girl, I'd known enough to say I was from Tama; it set me apart. Most of my friends had been born across the river at the big hospital in Omaha. They never treated me like an outsider, but I felt like one, a little.

Pulled along by Dad in his doomed pursuit of the stability he'd lost, I took this outside feeling with me; it accompanied me everywhere I went. I came to resent it. Wherever we were, it seemed, everybody else was local. Not me, not Lisa. There was a newness to every place that never wholly went away. It got worse every time we pulled up roots.

So when our first year in Madison ended and a second began, I allowed myself to begin feeling the pull of some small attachments I'd formed, and to stop forgetting things as soon as they happened. To let my heart begin the assembly of a new scrapbook. I still remember my friends from that time: Carol, whose mother was a professor at the university, and who was a transplant like me; Elsie, who knew how to swear in Norwegian; Damon, who I asked to the heavily chaperoned sixth-grade Sadie Hawkins dance, and who said yes. It felt like we'd finally come to a stop at last, but then somebody from the network of parents Dad had unearthed in Sioux Falls found our Wisconsin address somehow and sent a letter by registered mail saying there'd been a confirmed sighting of Michael Christopher at a former shoe store in Decorah. The records on the property were public and showed him taking out a year's lease. They'd been doing surveillance for two months to be sure. They were planning an intervention.

Dad took me with him; I waited in the car in the dark while the other families stormed the Wednesday evening Bible study, the deprogrammer from Chicago coordinating the abduction, his assistants emerging from the building two at a time, dragging parishioners by their arms, roughly slipping pillowcases over their heads and throwing them into the van. They got three out before the Christopher clan managed to barricade the door.

It was the climax of our seven-year search. I was twelve years old. The deprogrammer's van sped off, the remaining worshippers visible through the shoe store's glass door, crying and holding one another, unbathed, dressed in thrift store castoffs. Dad came back to the car and got in and started the engine, but he didn't say anything; I was a big girl, I could see for myself. Mom wasn't there.

After he died, years later, back in Crescent, I saved the surveillance tapes he'd gotten from the private investigator. They weren't hiding in a high cupboard or in a lockbox; he'd kept them in the entertainment center in the living room, like something you might watch on any idle evening. His clothes I drove across the river to the Goodwill on North Seventy-eighth; they might have gone to a vintage store in the Old Market by then, and fetched a decent price. They were so well preserved, relics of a simpler time. Surely they were worth something, but I felt a need to empty the house, quickly and methodically. It wasn't the house I'd lived in as a child. But Crescent is small. The house my mother'd left behind forever one Christmas was only a few blocks away. I stood in my father's room sorting his things into piles and tried to remember what our family had been like. But clear memories wouldn't come; everything blurred. I couldn't even make out their faces. It was like someone had scribbled over them in black marker, or wrapped them in shrouds.

The rest of his effects went to people from the church: old ladies who'd known my father when he was young. I thanked them for making it easier, and they helped me find boys from the high school to help with the furniture. I stood by while they worked, watching the house grow empty, the last remaining traces of my family vanishing into the gleam of things swept clean. It felt strange to be helping this work along, but the drive within me was instinctual, as natural to me as the brownness of my hair and eyes. When we had finished I headed back through Iowa alone.

At my apartment in Nevada, and then, later, at the Collins farmhouse I bought by pooling Dad's life insurance money with the proceeds from the Crescent house, I watched the surveillance tapes, night after night. They were hypnotic. They calmed me somehow, kept me centered. The anonymity of the people at the bus stops and around the bonfires at the trash dumps or behind the bowling alleys . . . there was a sort of hope in it, a gathering of possibilities that could never be dispelled entirely, because the names of the faces in the frame were lost forever. They could have been anybody. There was no way to say who they were or were not. They were free.

In their untrackable freedom I located a place to store something I had carried with me since Christmas of 1972, something whose need for space grew greater every year. I found a second VCR at a yard sale and began collecting moments from the endless time-stamped hours of my father's fruitless search. If you learn to look hard enough, you can find stories in seemingly impenetrable tableaus. Street scenes. Parking lots. People waiting for a bus.

I made a few friends: people who were drawn to me, to my steady strength, to my knack for making any place I stood feel like a permanent shelter. I preserved their stories, and when they had no stories, I gave them stories they could call their own, stories I trust they have carried with them in their travels beyond my reach, and I made of these stories a permanent record on tape. I filled in the parts I couldn't know or needed to change with bits and pieces of other people's stories: from the movies, I mean. But they all seemed to lead me to the same place. No attempt to change the outcome found purchase, however adept I became at splicing and cutting and smoothing transitions.

I left all this to ferment in the place where the people on Dad's tapes had gone: the great nowhere, the land whose air assumes the familiarity of whatever surroundings it finds. But it was never far from me, I learned. It was contained, but still curious. Left to guess at the dark around it, it became subject to simple metabolic laws of action and reaction. When it all burst free from its tank at the house in Collins, I sold the place quickly through a broker, said a hard goodbye to yet another friend I'd never see again, and finally came home.

In the basement, just outside the darkroom, Emily hung her freshly developed prints on a clothesline: she'd finished a roll in Tama after their plans fizzled. She was glad there'd been no confrontation; there'd been that woman waving at them from the upstairs window, and they'd waved back uncertainly, but then continued right on down the street, as if they had business elsewhere and had only pulled up because they'd seen an open spot. Nobody wants to be a pest, or bring up unpleasant memories. It was nice just to spend the day taking pictures of old buildings.

They wouldn't be there forever, the old buildings. Iowa seemed less bloodthirsty about its past than California, but she'd seen all the construction along the highway on the way in from Collins: mini-malls and motels, spaces for chain restaurants and cell phone stores. It's in the nature of the landscape to change, and it's in the nature of people to help the process along; there's no getting around it. It's the same everywhere in the end.

Still, when she considered her best shot from that morning—the old Tama Bank & Trust building, gray and imposing above the downtown square—she wondered what she'd already missed, what had gone missing from Iowa before she ever got there. There is no way of knowing. That's what pictures are for, after all: to stand in place of the things that weren't left behind, to bear witness to people and places and things that might otherwise go unnoticed.

It was so nice to have this hobby in retirement. There was so much to think about if you just gave yourself the time, even in places most people couldn't find on a map.

ACKNOWLEDGMENTS

This is a book largely about mothers, and it would be a grave oversight not to thank my own mother, Mary Noonan, who always encouraged me in my writing, and gave to me, for my seventh birthday, a Royal typewriter, vintage 1936 or so, which set me on my way. Without that old Royal: who knows?

Thanks to everyone working and studying in Building 4 here at Golden Belt: it's a pleasure and an inspiration to share this space with you.

Sean McDonald is my editor, and offers the gentlest, best suggestions, opening onto places I could never have found by myself: thank you!

Chris Parris-Lamb believed I could write books before I did. Neither this book nor the one before it could have been written without you. I am in your debt.

John Hodgman offered invaluable observations about this book during its writing, and great encouragement; how far astray it might have gone without your words of insight and support. Thank you!

Donna Tartt, you've been my steady companion in keeping the focus where it belonged as I wrote this book: a true confidant and a constant source of comfort and inspiration. Thank you, a dozen times over.

Thanks, too, to Steve Pietsch, Michael Ganzeveld, Lynsi Heldt, Lisa Chavanothai, Sarah Jane Gelner, Laura Lavender, and the many Iowans whose first or last names I borrowed for this book: only one of you, Steve, knew I was working on anything at all in this vein, but you were all with me in memory as I wrote.

And finally, to Lalitree Darnielle, née Chavanothai, mother of my sons and first hearer of these pages, through whom I first came to know Iowa, recurring thanks, here and in all that may follow.